MADNESS
&
MONSTERS

AN ANTHOLOGY OF CREEPY STORIES

PHILIP A. LEE

ぢ 7 ፀ

DAYTON, OHIO

WWW.PHILIPLEEWRITING.COM

Edited by Bill Bicknell
Cover and interior art by Michael Martin
Cover design by Matt Heerdt

First paperback edition: August 2014

ISBN 978-0-9911259-2-0 (paperback)
ISBN 978-0-9911259-1-3 (ebook)

LCCN: 2013920949

For Carrie,
who makes darkened corners a little less scary

Words, like angels, are powers which have invisible power over us . . . personal presences which have whole mythologies: genders, genealogies . . . histories, and vogues; and their own guarding, blaspheming, creating, and annihilating effects.

—James Hillman, psychologist

A man who has not passed through the inferno of his passions has never overcome them.

—Carl Jung, psychoanalyst

TABLE OF CONTENTS

FOREWORD

BY BILL BICKNELL

Normal, healthy adults don't believe in monsters . . . *necessarily*. The word "monsters" calls to mind a variety of images—bogeymen lurking under beds or in closets, Lovecraftian horrors lying in wait beneath the sea, shambling automatons from a mad scientist's lab. We read about these beasts, we shiver a bit, and we laugh. They're scary, sure, but it's not as if they're *real*.

Philip A. Lee doesn't deal in these sorts of monsters, but the beasts in his book will unsettle you in different ways. Instead, Philip is a master of parallels; when he holds the mirror up to nature, something disturbing crawls out of it.

What horrors await a priest who seeks the secrets of his guardian angel? What has transformed an old friend into an unknowable cipher? What mysteries hide within a discarded set of toys? And what fate awaits a supernatural temptress who finds herself questioning her very nature?

Within these stories and more—some of them magical, some of them conventional—monstrous truths stand as stark parallels to what is seemingly good . . . or simply mundane. How Philip's protagonists face these challenges will determine what fates await them. Some may find strength or validation; others will only find madness.

But regardless of the result, the monsters of *Monsters & Madness*—creatures of myth, of mind, and of flesh—will leave you squirming. You may not believe in monsters, but the stories in this collection might make you stare long and hard at the mirror, wondering where the creatures are really hiding.

INTRODUCTION

If you're wondering why this book is described on the cover as an anthology collection of "creepy stories" rather than "horror stories," here's your answer.

I've never been a fan of the kind of horror movies that rely on things jumping out at you when it's dead quiet, the kind that go for a "real" scare after the fake "Oh, it's just you" scare, or the ones that rely on copious amounts of gore and viscera solely to elicit shock or revulsion from the audience. Instead, I've always admired the kind of movies that drench the story in a well-crafted ambiance. Think of walking into a poorly lit mansion and seeing the owner's collection of porcelain dolls, all of which are staring at you. Think of that neighbor who doesn't seem all there, the one that's always in his backyard at night and watches you when you get out of your car. Think of that old, musty basement when the light bulb's burnt out and the door closes behind you.

In my opinion, these types of scenarios are far more powerful than pure shock factor. People exposed to violence and bloodshed can become inured to it after awhile, but that soft scritching coming from behind the closet door, the whistle coming from a badly sealed doorframe, the tapping of a leafless branch against a windowpane— these things will always put a chill down one's spine.

This idea dovetails into true horror being a deeply personal thing. Some people are so afraid of spiders that they need someone else to kill them, while others give spiders the bottom of their shoe without thinking twice about it. Some people can be bored by a slasher film while others will curl up into a ball at a specific scene, despite the inherent suspension of disbelief involved when watching a movie.

Because horror is intensely personal, it's probably no surprise that, of all the protagonists in this collection, only one has a name. This wasn't a deliberate choice while I was writing these stories, but in retrospect it demonstrates a fundamental truth that these sorts of things could happen to anyone, that each narrator is an everyman capable of encountering monsters or madness at any time, around any corner.

When reading through this collection, remember that what scares you might not necessarily scare someone else. For every person who suffers from arachnophobia, there's someone else with a boot and a grudge against spiders.

PHILIP A. LEE
22 OCTOBER 2013

WHEN COMETH THE ANGEL

When a faltering wagon cart suddenly hits a rut in the cobble and misses crushing you by mere inches, that, I always told my granddaughter Imogen, is your guardian angel shoving the cart aside. When the rheumatic fever or the typhoid plagues the body yet does not kill you, that is because your guardian angel fought the pathogens on your behalf and returned your soul to health. Anything heathens attribute to good fortune—a windfall, a close brush with death, a chance reunion of old friends—that is your guardian angel manipulating the course of fate into favorable trade winds.

These beings, I would tell Imogen, meet reality for but a moment, only long enough to kiss their charges with divine love before returning to their own plane.

I have known of my guardian angel's existence ever since I was six years old. My mother claimed the fever from the pox had addled my mind, but I could see my protector through bleary, rheumy eyes, if only for a moment. Phantom fingers embraced my cheeks, and when I looked up, I saw the most beautiful creature I could ever imagine: milky skin, feminine limbs with masculine power, and the most wondrous crystalline eyes filled with the softest kindness and the hardest resolve.

Six years later, this wondrous creature kept runaway hansom horses from trampling me. At thirty-three, it averted German bombs so their blast destroyed my pagan neighbor's house instead. Some considered me a lucky fellow, but I would tell them luck had nothing to do with the countless near-scrapes I endured to reach this ripe old age. A secret benefactor was responsible for my success, I would say to them, and they would immediately ask my silent partner's name.

This set me to wondering: did my angel possess a name? And if so, how could I learn what it was?

My colleagues at the university, they laughed when I broached this rather peculiar conjecture. My associates and I, we have always argued about the value of what lies beyond our eyes. As learned men of repute and tenure, most of them considered the idea rubbish, but I always argued devil's advocate in favor of the preternatural merely to stimulate discourse amongst my peers. I would ask them about miraculous occurrences that had happened to them, things they could not explain away by scientific reasoning. They said it was chance. Fortune. Fate.

In the furtherance of my studies, it came to my attention that pagans throughout history have repeatedly attempted to call forth demons. They seek not to control or subdue them but to gain their knowledge or perhaps curry their favor. In 1909, Aleister Crowley and Victor Neuberg claimed to have successfully summoned a demon, one whom many pagan scholars believe to be the archdemon Satan himself, and that they had stolen its secrets. As a counterpoint, I came across many tales of people communicating with their guardian angels during deep meditation or near-death experiences, but these were the angels of paganism, not the divine messengers of God Almighty. I read through any theological tome in the university library that contained any reference to angels or demons, and not once did I find mention of someone attempting to call forth a brother of Michael or a cousin of Gabriel.

What, I asked myself, was the loftier ideal: to probe the depths for Belial's secrets or to touch the very mind of God?

I partook of Eucharist the next Sabbath and shared my private thoughts with the priest in his offices after Mass. He eyed me with intense scrutiny, and for a moment, I thought he would prescribe penance from the look on his face.

"Be careful what you wish for, Doctor," he said. "The mind of God is too powerful a thing for earthen vessels such as we."

When I explained that I only wished to commune with my guardian angel, he waggled a finger and said, "My child, what makes you believe God does not know His angels better than He knows us? They are His first, perfect in every way, as He is. We are His flawed creatures, and to touch something so sacred could bring disastrous repercussions to he who is prideful enough to believe it can be done."

I left the cathedral with a famine of ideas in my head and an emptiness in my heart. I had grown so enamored of the notion that having its very integrity impugned by the only soul I considered a friend in the matter left me a broken and disconsolate spirit. Was it not the goal of every good Catholic to better know the mind of God? Was it not my good, Christian duty to strive to understand His ways?

After three months' time, I felt I was building another Tower of Babel, like I was sailing across the Sea of Galilee in a storm, never to find the other side. I called upon the powers that be to help me find a way. And lo! in the midst of reading the Holy Scriptures, I received an epiphany.

From the Prophet Isaiah, chapter fourteen: "How art thou fallen from heaven, O Lucifer, son of the morning!"

Angels were demons who had not yet fallen and thus could be called forth in similar ways.

In utmost secrecy, I read as much as I could on subjects no Christian would ever dream of touching to find the truth. Many books I purchased from shadowed figures in dark alleys—witches and practitioners of magic that did not wish open persecution. Forgotten, annotated books about séances, symbols, and arcane incantations. Handwritten treatises of the nature and disposition of all known demonic entities. After several months of arduous research, I knew more about ancient religions and magic than I would have thought prudent ten years before. Pick a mantra from the Vedas, a *galdr* chant from *Runes of the Nine Worlds*, a spell from a Hermetic grimoire—I could recite them all.

For each pagan concept, I found a morally superior reciprocal. Death became life. Darkness became light. Sacrificial blood became blessed wine. Occult incantation became Scripture quotation.

Still I went to Mass each Sunday, if only to remind myself that I was fulfilling my good Christian duty, albeit in ways the priest did not understand. I read the Good Book as much as I read Crowley's *The Vision and the Voice*. I wanted to know how he had enticed Beelzebub and thus learn how to bait a true, Christian angel of protection.

I planned the ritual for Easter Sunday instead of Samhain, and I began my preparations at first light instead of waiting for nightfall. The flowers and grass of my garden were a perfect substitute for a summoner's candlelit pentagram; my Holy Bible became my grimoire.

The triangle of evocation I drew in the sod of my summoning ground represented the Holy Trinity; there lay no maleficence in that. And the wine used to seal the triangle had been blessed and taken from the Church. Nothing unholy there. I had spent a fortnight drafting an incantation of my own based on the Scriptures. Latin replaced the Enochian summoning language and thus removed all sense of paganism from my work.

From a blessed flame, I began the ceremony. I had stolen it also from the cathedral, having carried it away in secret after it was blessed for Vespers and covered it with a tin to ensure it would not blow out before I could begin. With it, I lit the paschal candle and dropped five grains of incense into the flame.

Amidst the heady scent, I pierced the candle with a knife five times, the stabs representing the five wounds of the Christ. I lifted the column of wax and dipped its base into a silver basin of holy water, also blessed and taken in secret from my congregation. This ablutionary act symbolized the Christ's baptism and was intended to purify my soul from any evil that might have seeped into it, any contact taint from the books of darkness I had secretly been studying.

With a deep breath, I spoke my invocation to the sky.

"*In nomine Patris, et Filii, et Spiritus Sancti,*" I began. "May the Holy Ghost bless this mortal place with the gift of knowledge and communion."

And thus set in motion events I was powerless to stop.

Spring winds blew while I meditated upon Scripture and threatened to extinguish the blessed candle. The sun darkened while I called forth the name of God. More than any other desirable thing, I wished to know my guardian angel as I knew others, so I persisted. I wanted to touch the sacred as He has touched the rest of this world. I wanted to prove my fellows wrong.

After a long passage of time, the light through my eyelids waned. Night hailed me when I chanced to look. How long had it been since I had started? Minutes? Hours? The daylight had expired much sooner than I had anticipated, and the biting wind grew all the colder.

Only by the melting candle flame and the silvery moonlight could I see. In my ruminations, I noticed I had scuffed away a portion of the evocation triangle with my shoe during my meditations; this more than likely was the cause for my failure thus far. From the flagon of wine, I carefully poured more onto the broken triangle to reseal it, but as I did so, some splashed against my fingers. It was warm despite the wind. When I looked closer, I saw that it was not wine but blood. Actual blood.

I am not a man of faint heart, but this sight so disturbed my rational mind that I gasped and accidentally dropped the flagon. It shattered into a thousand pieces, inexplicably dousing fresh blood onto my flower garden, just outside the triangle. Any pagan magician would have found this spilt blood outside of the triangle a disastrous omen; I took it for a favorable sign. At the Last Supper, the Christ had turned the wine into his blood, and on Easter Sunday, no less, this was a fortuitous portent.

The splattered crimson quickened my faith, so I continued my spiritual quest with renewed fervor. The recitations of Scripture came faster than I could speak, the words a muddle in my mouth.

From the epistles of Saint Paul: *My grace is sufficient for thee: for my strength is made perfect in weakness.*

From the prophet Jeremiah: *Call unto me, and I will answer thee, and show thee great and mighty things, which thou knowest not.*

My head became hot from the strain. My heart raced.

After a time, I felt prickles dotting across my forehead. My side soon ached as though I had run harder than accustomed to. Then my ankles started to hurt. At first, I thought this was because I had been sitting on them for far too long, but not until I felt stabbing pain pierce my wrists did I realize what had happened.

When I opened my eyes, I saw that the blood from the flagon had not only splashed the ground outside the triangle, but it had stained my wrists, my shirt, and my shoes. I had manifested the stigmata, the holy sign of the Catholic faith, the truest personification of sympathy with the Christ's suffering. But as I gently touched the representative wounds, I winced; they ran as deep as though they were real.

Each beat of my heart pumped more of my lifeblood into the ground. Crimson filled the triangle of the Trinity and poured out through the design until the lines could no longer be seen.

I recall little of what transpired past this moment, but suffice it to say I remember losing consciousness. But this unconsciousness was not that of the comatose: each and every thing happening around me I could see. I could walk around my own body, mutilated with the five holy marks, and see the hideous face the ceremony had bestowed upon me—wild eyes, arched brows, mouth twisted in malevolent glee. For the longest time, I thought I was dead, that I drifted through the ether towards purgatory, heaven, or—God forbid—hell. But my physical body still breathed, still heaved up and down.

And then the most incredible light assaulted me from behind. This was not "white light" as a physicist might define. No, it was *whiter* than white, whiter than white could ever be, if you take my meaning. I was blinded but had no eyelids to close. I felt naked in the light, and when I turned, not even my ethereal hands could clothe that terrible, shameful sensation.

Amidst the blazing white, it stood before me with naked arms outstretched. Hair the color of gold bathed its shoulders, and its open eyes radiated the same color as the blinding light, as if the eye sockets bored holes right through its head to reveal the pure whiteness behind it.

And it was as beautiful as I had remembered as a child. For a moment, it looked like a woman unclothed, the most extravagant female form I have ever seen in my time on this earth. Had I still been in my body, I would have fallen prey to all manner of fleshly lusts, all unspeakable debauchery and depravity. Then it became male, then female, slowly shifting back and forth between the two extremes before settling on pure androgyny.

Ever so timidly, I asked the angel its name.

"My name," it said in such a dreamy, watery voice, "is Damien."

If my etymological roots served me well, "Damien," I recalled, meant "one who subdues."

A curious name for an angel.

I asked if it was my guardian angel, the one who had spared me from the pox, saved me from the runaway horses, deflected the Nazi bombs.

It nodded and beckoned me to come closer.

How could I refuse such beauty, such radiance? After all, if this had safely ushered me into my middle years, how could I not feel obligated by a debt of obedience? With a smile, I approached my divine savior and clasped hands with it. Its skin was softer than the most gentle baby flesh, and when it laughed, I felt the whole world lift from my shoulders.

Out of sincerest respect and, dare I say, love, I asked my angel what it wanted from me. After all, it had given me so much; anything I would offer in return could never hope to repay the debt I had accumulated in this life.

"Look into my eyes," Damien said. "Look deep into my eyes and you will know."

Regardless of how much as I wanted to look into the light, those empty eyes unsettled me. Anyone faced with an eyeless skull would feel the same, but the light itself was so entrancing. The closer I came to those fathomless eyes, the more I realized they were not eyes at all. Its eye sockets did indeed tunnel straight through the creature's head, through brain and bone alike.

I recoiled, but the angel's grip remained firm. Its thin, white lips pursed into a hard line. "You would do well to obey," it said, its voice no longer the soft comfort it had once been. "Look deeper."

And while I gazed frightfully into the holes, the light I saw through the angel's empty eyes changed into a reddish orange fire. Then, with a gasp, it became the color of blood. Through the angel's eyeholes, I stared straight at the blood splattered across the now-dying flowers in my garden. The wine-turned-blood and the scarlet still issuing from my mortal coil had completely obliterated the summoning triangle in the grass.

"See here what you have done," boomed the angel, a hint of pleasure in its voice, "and remember. Because of you, I have fallen like Lucifer, and your ritual of ignorance has freed me into the world."

When I pulled away from the eyes, the angel's face was no longer beautiful. Its soft skin was rough, its limbs twisted into dead tree branches, and its ugly, misshapen face lost every hint of the kindness it once possessed. But its eyes were still holes to nowhere.

In tears I told the angel I would banish it back to the realm from whence it came, having read ways of banishing.

"You cannot banish what you cannot control," said the angel.

It smiled. The world blackened, and I felt my spirit being sucked back into my body. I heard laughter and my own screams, and then I knew no more.

It is said that bad luck and ill fortune befell Aleister Crowley for the rest of his life because he had not properly banished the demon he had summoned. Now I know how the poor man felt. Often I wonder if he knew how much strife and evil in the world his personal demon had caused. Had he sat there and watched his demon destroy everything he'd ever held dear, perverted every grain of truth in his life's work, and sown seeds of discord throughout the world that led to untamable conflict?

When I awoke in the sanitarium, my heart fell into utter despair. I had no inkling of what the angel had planned to do with its newfound freedom, but the mere thought of the lurid machinations it was capable of sent me into a terrible panic. Nurses would often burst in and find me writhing on the floor, foaming at the mouth, and threatening to swallow my tongue.

Only my dearest Imogen visited me. Each time my granddaughter stopped by, I could sense my guardian angel's growing agitation. The last time I ever saw her or my tormentor, I watched helplessly as the fallen angel followed her out of my room.

EXEUNT

My roommate—the Broadway buff—suggests I go to a play with him; this is his first mistake.

"It's actually a musical," he says. "Supposed to be really funny."

The title sounds unfamiliar to me—*Mortem Dux* . . . Latin, I believe—so Roomie confirms it's more of a local, word-of-mouth performance than some big, nationally known production.

I relent out of sheer curiosity. He takes me to some theater I've never heard of, this place downtown whose box office you can only get to by a rear entrance off the main drag. The building looks old even from the outside. The moment we wander inside, I wonder if the dusty smell hanging in the air is actually asbestos giving me lung cancer.

The theater itself is a tad small—probably only seats a few hundred people or so. The rows of plush, wine-colored opera chairs have certainly seen some use over the years, but if the exterior of the building is any indication, this place won't be able to afford replacing their upholstery for some time. I swear a small cloud of dust puffs up when I sit down in my seat. Now I'm no theater aficionado—I don't spell it "theatre" like Roomie does—but the stage itself has also seen better days. The gilding on the angelic woodwork framing the stage has already begun to peel, and the stage surface is covered in the scuffs and scratches of countless performers' footwear.

Old architecture is one thing, but overall I am not impressed. In deference to Roomie's love of live theater, I keep this to myself.

The seats are pretty packed when the show starts. The lights dim and performers come onto the stage dressed in some kind of Victorian-era couture. Suits and dresses, smoking jackets and ascots, bustles and petticoats. One of them is a guy I could swear I graduated high school with.

In the musical this proletarian guy courts a woman of nobility—problem number one. He's twenty-something; she's fortyish—problem number two. He runs afoul of the law, and she ends up marrying some old Duke of Whatever—problem number three. But, for all its flaws, my friend was right.

It's damned funny.

I don't really remember any of the characters' names or, honestly, how the thing ended up because I'm laughing so hard. The cast would clearly never make it into professional theater, but I cannot help but wonder why such a great piece wasn't advertised in the newspaper.

During the applause, the old duke moves to center stage, and the rest of the cast forms a circle around him. In a moment of surrealism, the young lover pulls a knife on the duke. There is blood. Lots of blood. No one screams but the duke. The suddenness of the gore brings bile rising in my throat, yet I'm too busy laughing to vomit. This is clearly part of the production, one last over-the-top sight gag.

Then the avenged young lover and the elderly matron live happily ever after. Once the last song-and-dance number finishes, the entire cast of villagers and nobility lines up on stage with smiles and laughter, the young proletarian lover with dull red comically splattered on his chimneysweep jacket.

The dead duke does not return for the curtain call. *Mortem Dux*— The Duke's Death. Fitting title, I guess.

Since we both liked it so much, we linger around afterwards so Roomie can congratulate some of the stars, including some guy he swears he went to college with. Long after the other patrons have made the theater a ghost town, the blood-splattered young lover approaches us.

"You want to join the cast week after next?" he casually asks Roomie.

The star doesn't ask me. He doesn't even look at me.

Roomie jumps at the chance; I just roll my eyes. Not every Broadway buff will make a good actor. Or a singer. Roomie's shower voice can kill babies.

Back home, while Roomie's on the phone talking at some would-be girlfriend, I'm looking up the place in the Yellow Pages. Let your fingers do the walking.

Tennis Courts. Tents. Theatres-Cinema. Theatres-Stage.

Okay. Playhouses. Dinner theatres. Opera Associations . . .

There is no listing for this place. None. Come to think of it, I didn't even get a program.

Roomie gets off the phone with his girl toy. "You wanna see that musical again?" he says.

He does not have to specify *which* musical.

"I'll be in it," he says. "I'll be playing that young bloke chasing the Matron."

Then he points to his phone and says he's bringing his girlfriend, his toy.

The toy in question turns out to be this auburn-haired minx that he knows I can't stand. She cannot shut up. Always talking and going on about nothing for hours on end. And I'm stuck with her for the whole evening since her beau will be in the cast.

When Roomie's debut arrives, Minx is quiet as a mouse, other than the laughter. Guffawing all throughout the show, she obviously thinks the play is even funnier than I did the first time. Roomie is indeed the young lover, and honest to Gandhi, he's not half as bad as I expected him to be.

The cast is all different this time. Someone else plays the part of the duke this week, but he's at least old enough to portray His Grace, the Duke of Whatever.

Right before curtain call, right before the final song-and-dance number, Roomie pulls the knife while everyone's still laughing at the last joke. *Mortem Dux*. So much blood for such a small knife. So much blood. It's ridiculous.

But Minx is ecstatic. To everyone who'll listen, she says, "That's my man! That's my love muffin!"

The theater empties out again, and only my roommate returns to the abandoned stage. He asks Minx if she liked it. Then he asks her if she wants to be a member of the production.

When she doesn't answer, he says, "There's a leading role coming up soon, and I think you'd be perfect for it."

He doesn't mention a word to me, the ungrateful bastard.

Giggling, Minx jumps at the chance.

This is apparently our new hobby.

Two weeks later, I'm in the stands alone amongst strangers, watching the play, worrying about asbestos. Roomie isn't the young lover tonight, and for some reason the story has changed a little. This time it's about a younger woman—played by Minx—being envious of the young lover's cradle-robbing affair.

But hey, it's still funny, especially with all the stage antics. When Minx stabs the older woman out of jealousy—*Mortem Matrona*, I guess— I can't help but laugh because of the cheesiness of it all. The theater blood that drowns out the asbestos scent. The gurgling, bubbly sounds when Minx pretends to slit the matron's throat. The cascade of stage blood completely dyeing Matron's whole outfit.

Afterward, Minx asks me to join the cast.

How can I say no? This has become like our favorite movie. Our new obsession. Our very own *Rocky Horror*.

Backstage, paint peels from the walls, and piles of fallen ceiling debris are swept into unused corners. Everything is just as asbestos-ridden as the rest of the theater, but I do not care if I get lung cancer. It's my turn now.

There are no real rehearsals. Aside from the main gist of the story and the central melodies, every performance is improvised. During the show, whatever I say or sing seems appropriate for the situation. I am the young lover now, estranged by age and husbands. My only clearly defined task is to stab my rival, the oldest member of the cast, with the rubber stage knife I'm given.

Everything goes fine until the finale. I work myself up into my role. Hot blood pulses through my temples. Sweat and stage lights sting my eyes. The man before me—His Grace, the esteemed Duke of Whatever—I hate more than anything else, more than asbestos, more than lung cancer, more than silicosis.

"*Damn your love!*" I scream at him. "Damn you *and* your filthy whore!"

And I lunge at him with the knife. Amidst all the laughter, amidst all the violent applause at my having finally achieved my long deserved vengeance.

The Duke's blood is warm. It smells like magnets or stale pennies. It is not stage blood. The knife is not a prop.

My stomach flutters. Bile gushes up my esophagus, and I have to fight down the urge to vomit at the gore bathing my clothes, splattering the stage, my fellow actors and actresses. But Roomie and Minx, their eyes light up with approval. My bloody stiletto clatters to the stage, and people are applauding the Duke's comeuppance.

But they don't know that I'm a murderer. A goddamned murderer. *Mortem Dux.*

"Welcome to the club," Roomie tells me back by Wardrobe after the curtain call. Minx, the Matron, the villagers, they all nod and smile.

"It's your turn to go out there and invite someone to join us," Minx tells me. Just like Lover invited Roomie, like Roomie invited her, like she invited me. It's like vampires: only a cast member can make someone else a cast member.

I hesitate. The remnants of my murderous fit still linger in my head. The Duke's pleading eyes consumes my every thought.

"Everyone dies," Roomie says. "Normal people die and are

forgotten, but dying onstage, before riotous applause . . ." He slow-claps his velvet gloves together, and his eyes roll back into his head as he shudders. "That will make us *immortal.*"

"Laughter is the spell," Matron says, coming a step closer. "Laughter is what sobers the audience into seeing what they want to see."

"But I'm a murderer," I plead with them.

"Everyone wants to be immortal," Roomie says. "You only helped the Duke on his road to godhood."

"The show must go on," says Matron. The rest of the cast has drawn uncomfortably close, blocking my escape. "You are either with us or against us. There's no turning back."

"And if you choose to go against us," one of the villagers threatens, "your own play will end long before its third act."

Silently, I leave Wardrobe and wander into the audience. Knowing full well one of these snot-nosed punks who stayed behind will become another hapless murderer in short order, I end up recruiting one anyway, an enthusiastic young girl with the stink of "freshman drama major" all over her. At our next performance, she ushers our oldest member into the ranks of gods while I stand and watch—not as myself but as Chorus Member 3.

Matron receives her own glory a few weeks later; Chorus Member 2—Yours Truly—cheers her death along with the audience.

Every time I perform, I watch our newest member take the life of another without motive or malice. Every time I walk onto the stage, I draw closer to my own death, my own immortality. Each time someone is murdered, their soul departs to the sound of the merriment and gaiety of a crowd who sees only what they are deceived into seeing.

This circle continues for so long that each death is expected. Before a Matron or a Duke's final performance, we don't say goodbye. Instead we pat them on the shoulder and say, "Break a leg," remind them not to say "Macbeth" on stage.

No longer do I fear asbestos or lung cancer. I already know how my play will end.

Silver hair peppers my temples by the time some young blonde piss kills Roomie in a crimson spray. Two weeks later some little, sandy-haired prick murders Minx in a ghastly flood of intestines. Everyone in the crowd assumes it is a Tony-worthy special effects job.

The show after that, it's my turn.

I wonder, is lung cancer really so bad?

I have no other choice but to attend my final performance. Acting is a hopelessly addictive drug, a powerful escape. Being someone else is such a release from the nightmare. And the show is really hysterical, regardless of which side of the stage you're on, regardless of the truth behind the façade.

But then, for the first time, I actually look at the knife that has created so many gods and goddesses. Not rubber. Not a prop. Cold, hard steel.

My murder weapon.

I panic. I don't come on stage when my final scene is about to begin. I'm already out the window by Wardrobe, down the rickety fire escape stairs. I'm out of the alley. Down the street. In the office of the local precinct.

"Check the theater," I tell the cops. There are hundreds of murderers, recruiting a new one every other week. A death cult posing as a theater group. A suicide ring. This has gone on for decades.

Two policemen follow me, but as soon as I turn in the alley, the box office window is gone. Where it had once been, only bricks and mortar remain.

"Nothing here," the cops say. "Looks like nothing's ever been here."

And they are right. For the first time, I see the building code notice. Tears stain the alley cement. I am crying so hard I cannot breathe.

My entire life has been thrown away on someone else's joke, someone else's conspiracy. As I stare at a condemned building, all I have left are the regrets and memories of my deceased friend and his innocent lover.

This is when I feel a subtle pinprick against my ribcage. I look down and one of the cops is pulling the stage knife out of me. There is so much blood. Stage blood, makeup effects, I keep telling myself. It really doesn't hurt that bad.

The officer pulls off his cap. It is the new recruit, the one who was supposed to kill me in the third act. His partner is last month's Lover.

My head reels. As I stagger and hit the wall, I notice people watching. From behind dumpsters, down fire escapes, and out of open windows, beggars in Cockney rags and aristocrats in bustles and smoking jackets emerge from the woodwork to witness my murder.

Mortem Dux.

The play had never stopped. And I am bleeding out on a stage from which there will be no curtain call.

None of them will help me. No one will call an ambulance. There is nothing left but to go out with a bang.

"Alas, I am slain," I say and collapse against the dirty brick wall.

From the gutter, I can barely hear the crescendo of applause over my own heartbeat.

I look out at all of my stage friends.

"Break a leg," one of them says.

"Be careful not to say 'Macbeth,'" mouths another.

They will talk about this for years. The defector, the one who tried to write himself out of his own story, the one who finally brought their work to the outside world.

My fingers are cold. I can't feel my toes anymore.

But I smile, regardless.

I will be immortal.

UNDONE

They say college changes people, but ever since what happened to James, I can't help but think how no one really understands how true that statement is.

Everyone knows at least one person who shipped off to an out-of-state school or spent a few years abroad serving in the military, and when they came back home to Podunkville after seeing the wide world, they were different. Older. More mature. Sometimes these old friendships die off: those coming back home have changed too much, or the lines of communication just aren't there anymore. Well, James was like that. I could see it in his eyes the moment he pulled into his parents' driveway after graduating from MIT. But with James, it was something else entirely.

Before college, we were inseparable. In kindergarten, we bonded over our mutual love of sci-fi action figures—the more guns, the better, we always said—and when we got older, we both followed college football with a passion. Once we hit middle school, we both knew with childish certainty that we'd either end up in the military or the NFL together.

Needless to say, neither of those things happened. Somewhere along to road to high school graduation, James decided he would make a better engineer or civil servant than a ball player, regardless of how many touchdowns he scored for our varsity team. I didn't have the kind of money or smarts to get into MIT like he did, and having seen countless war movies throughout my adolescence, I'd discovered that the prospect of enlisting in the actual military scared the living daylights out of me, so that was out as well. He'd move on to greater things, and me—well, I knew I'd be stuck living day to day until he came home to visit.

Our last night together before he shipped out to Massachusetts, we hung out at his place and spent the evening watching and discussing two of our favorite things: a retrospective on OSU vs. Michigan games and the schlocky *Starship Troopers* movie. We both cheered when the Buckeyes beat the Wolverines in the '06 matchup, and later on we both rooted for Carmen Ibanez to die a horrible death in the movie, even though we knew she wouldn't.

Some things, like football rivalries or movies, don't ever change, but people change all the time, and not always for the best—and not always in ways you can see.

Every Christmas and summer when James came home to visit— "slumming," I always called it—he seemed a little different than before, which I expected given the time and the distance. Each year, he sounded less excited when I'd tell him about how the Buckeyes were doing in their conference, but I never once heard him talk about MIT's football team.

At the end of his junior year, James married his college sweetheart Emily. To this day I remember being alone with him in the side room while waiting for the wedding to start. Given that he was about to say "I do" less than an hour later, he struck me as a little too confident at the time. As best man, I felt it was my duty to ask him if something was wrong—I mean, what groom, no matter how much he loves his fiancée, goes to the altar without sweating bullets or being one step away from melting into a puddle?—but for some reason, I didn't.

Sometimes I think if I'd have just asked him right then, when he should've been his most vulnerable, none of what came after would've happened. But guys just don't talk about emotions and stuff like that, or at least society has trained us to believe that we shouldn't. Screw that, I say. If I could go back and change only one moment in my life, it would've been to ask him what was wrong.

After getting his B.S. in Engineering, James and Emily stayed at their Cambridge apartment over the summer and finally moved back home right in early fall. To celebrate his homecoming, his new job, and the beginning of college football season, me and a few other friends took him out to B-Dubs to watch the first game of the season on the big TV.

I spent the evening cheering on the Buckeyes, as did our other friends, but James . . . In the second quarter, I glanced over at him and saw that same look he had in his eyes right before he got married. While the rest of us hooted and hollered at the TV whenever our offense ran a good play, he just sat there in the booth and stared.

In the last thirty seconds of the game, Buffalo was down by six, and it was fourth-and-goal. Buffalo's quarterback passed the ball in a tight spiral to the wide receiver just a few yards from the end zone. The catch looked to be good . . . until one of the Ohio State safeties charged in from the side in what seemed like torturous slow-mo. The defensive back crashed into the receiver and shouldered him aside—

Interception! My friends and I went completely ballistic, whooping and cheering along with the rest of the restaurant patrons. Defense ran the ball all the way into the end zone, and the Buckeyes ended up winning by thirteen after making the extra point.

I looked over at James right as the Buckeyes scored the final touchdown, and he had this calm, neutral look on his face, like he was somewhere else. Now, in the past he'd never been much for punching holes in walls when Ohio State lost a game, but he always—*always*—showed at least some bit of dismay when plays went bad or calls didn't go our way.

After knocking back the last of his beer, he said, "Good game," and set his glass on the tabletop.

I didn't know what to make of it at the time.

A few days later, James, Emily, a couple other friends, and I were out at a local bar for dinner and drinks. One of the TVs was showing the evening news. The anchor was talking about some tax bill passing through the House, and a murmur rippled amongst our friends.

In early high school, James took a deep interest in political science, despite his leanings towards engineering. In addition to playing for varsity football, he was senior class vice president, excelled on debate team, and took part in the Model United Nations. To this day, I'm surprised he didn't go for a poli-sci degree. He always voted; always stayed informed; and when he'd visit during college breaks, he and I would talk about whatever shenanigans the government was up to at the time. But there in the bar that night? He just shrugged. *Shrugged.*

"Render unto Caesar, *et cetera*," he said and threw back a large swig of craft-brewed ale.

This apathy about football, about politics—it all reminded me of a documentary I once saw about a lady who'd survived severe brain trauma but was robbed of her ability to feel emotion. James struck me as being like that poor girl, only he could still smile, still laugh. But whatever intangible thing that had made James *James* was gone, and I had no idea how to coax it back to life.

Like an itch right behind my eyes that I could not scratch, I wanted to know what had happened to him, but I could not bring myself to ask. Something like "Hey, Jim, did you lose your ability to *feel?*" never struck me as something a friend should say.

The first piece of the puzzle came a month after his return home.

For as long as I had known James's mother Katharine, she always had a kind word and the same smile her genetics had passed on to her son. Whenever he would invite me over on the weekends during high school, she would feed us to bursting at dinner and make sure the pantry and fridge were stocked with snacks and beverages for later. She would always ask about my mother and sisters or how my part-time job at Burger King was going. Once James returned home from college, nothing much had changed other than me working a mundane office job rather than flipping burgers.

About a month after James graduated, James, Emily, and I found his mother lying on her couch, her skin pallid and blue-tinged. I stayed with them throughout the ordeal. I was there shortly before the EMTs arrived. I was there at the morgue and the medical examiner's office. I was there when the coroner shared the autopsy results. Nocturnal asphyxiation—James's mother had suffocated in her sleep.

The wake and burial were small and private. I don't remember many details about what was said in eulogy, but one single image burned itself in my mind.

Once most of the attendees had departed the funeral home to leave for the burial site, James stood alone before the open casket. His face was neither grim nor upset. He simply reflected upon the soft sheen of the casket's polished surface, blinked, and kissed his mother's forehead. Emily drew up beside him and placed a comforting arm around his shoulders. Once he was done, he turned and went back to the car without a single tear dampening his cheek.

The three of us went out for dinner and drinks the next evening. James sounded like nothing had happened. He spoke of his mother fondly, as though he might see her once he returned home. Emily and I only looked at each other and shrugged. He had to be bottling his emotions inside, but I could not detect any telltale signs of the five stages of grief rising to the surface. He didn't give in to irritability.

At the graveside, after the priest's benediction, I asked James if he missed his mother, and he shrugged. "Why wouldn't I?" he said without missing a beat, without any twinge of regret or melancholy staining his eyes.

As far as I could tell, business had already returned to normal for James.

Later that night, I decided to break my self-imposed friendship protocol. Emily had already gone inside to make ice cream when I stopped and confronted him on the front porch.

"Aren't you even going to mourn your own mother?" I asked a bit more harshly than I had intended. "She's not even cold in the ground, but you're acting like nothing's different."

And he smiled that same smile, the one that spoke volumes more than it displayed. Somewhere in that smile hid a kind of flippant disregard that bristled me the wrong way. "Why should I mourn?" he replied. "Mourning solves nothing. My mother had a good life, and nothing I do can bring her back. So why try?"

"There's nothing wrong with showing some emotion," I said. "It's only human."

"And what is 'human'?" he answered. "A descriptor we created to make us feel superior to animals. *All* beings feel pain; some just know how to manage it better than others. Just because we possess the physiology to cry doesn't mean we need to. Catharsis doesn't always solve everything. Transcendence does. Once you learn the secret, then sorrow and despair become trivialities."

I frowned. "Then what is this secret?"

"If I told you, it wouldn't be a secret," he said with an emotionless laugh. "Besides, I couldn't tell you even if I wanted to. My words wouldn't make any sense. The answer can only result from epiphany."

My head spun. What he said made some twisted sense but at the same time made no sense at all. "Fine," I said. "Just so long as you don't end up murdering someone when you eventually snap."

He grinned—not a smug or condescending look but the same friendly smile I had known since we were playing with action figures in the front yard. "Don't worry about me," he said. "I'm okay. Really."

I closed my eyes and shook my head.

We sat on his mother's couch with Emily and his Shih-Tzu Trixie and ate ice cream from his mother's bowls with his mother's silverware while watching movies on his mother's television. Everything in the house reminded me of her in some way. The kitchen, where she'd make us meals whenever I hung out. The living room, where we'd chat about my family. The backyard, where she kept her flower garden. The window she made me replace after I accidentally broke it with a baseball. Everywhere I turned resurrected another memory of her—some good, some bad—but James carried on like she was just in the other room.

This disgusted me to no end. James was still the lifelong friend I had grown up with, but some part of him was irrevocably different.

But *why?* More than anything I wanted to know. Somehow, I *had* to know. I had to!

Trixie bounded into my lap, licked my face, and settled down into my lap, creating a warm, white-and-brown blanket across my legs. As I stroked her soft fur and lulled her into sleep, I watched James's continued stoicism and hatched a desperate plan to make his stony exterior break.

The next weekend, I dropped by while Emily was out shopping at the mall. We spent most of the time talking about work and current events, but none of my carefully directed comments elicited any real response from him.

I was still shaking my head when he went to the bathroom, but his refusal to budge cemented my resolve to execute my plan.

From a small Tupperware container I'd been keeping in my pocket, I stirred some powdered rat poison into Trixie's food bowl and mixed it in with the gravy. Not enough poison to hurt her, mind—I'd done my homework—but just enough to get my point across.

Trixie wandered over to her water dish about the time James came back from the bathroom. She lapped up water with her little, pink tongue, but she bypassed the food bowl and again curled up on my lap. The remainder of the evening, I kept vigilant watch on her whenever she left my lap. I waited nervously for her to take a bite, but she never did. Perhaps she could smell the poison. I took this as a sign that I was making a grave mistake.

By the time I left, Trixie had fallen asleep in her bed by the back door, her bowl completely untouched. I went home that night shouldering considerable guilt and foolishness for what I had tried to do. Trixie hadn't gone near the bowl all day, so James would assume that particular can of dog food had gone bad and he'd throw it out.

The next morning Emily called me on the phone with hysteria in her voice.

"Trixie's dead," she told me.

My stomach lurched. There was no way I had done that. None. If Trixie *had* eaten some of the poison, she would've thrown up, maybe gotten a little sick, but not . . . I never intended to kill her. That's the God's honest.

When I arrived, James greeted me with his usual deadened smile and went about his business. Emily sat in front of Trixie's bed, rocking herself back and forth in front of the unmoving ball of white and brown fur.

"How did it happen?" I somehow found the courage to ask.

James shrugged with the greatest nonchalance I had ever seen in a grown man. "She choked on a piece of food," he said.

I could not help but wonder if Trixie had died from the poison or if she had legitimately choked to death on coincidence. I mean, accidents happens all the time, right? The result was the same either way, but James's indifferent performance didn't even so much as budge as the morning progressed.

He ate breakfast at the dining room table while Emily just cried an endless fount of tears. "I'd had her since I was sixteen," she told me in between sobs. "She was a puppy, the smallest little thing . . ."

And James just sat and had orange juice and cornflakes for breakfast. He was listening to his wife, of course, but not as intently as I. He should have been kneeling next to her like I was, maybe holding her close, and for God's sake shedding some tears! His stoicism would have won him the gold medal in the Neglectful Husband Olympics, but I doubt he even would have celebrated that victory.

Instead of burying Trixie in the backyard, Emily wanted her cremated, the ashes placed in an urn on the mantel. James probably would have gone to the vet with her, but a pet dying didn't qualify for bereavement leave. Fortunately, I was between work projects, and I couldn't bear the thought of her going by herself.

Emily reverently placed Trixie's prone form in a shoebox, and we left for the appointment. She stayed rather quiet on the way, but she was sobbing by the time she conferred with the vet. Not until the return trip—with Trixie's urn on her lap—was she able to say anything of consequence.

"You've known Jimmy for a long time," she said after a stretch of uncomfortable silence. "Have you . . . noticed anything different about him lately?"

Finally, someone else had seen it. I was no longer alone.

"I can't put my finger on it," she continued, "but he doesn't talk to me the way he used to. He's . . . distant. Detached."

"He still hasn't mourned his mother," I said.

"No. He . . ." She gesticulated with one hand then faced me. "It's almost like she's not dead to him. I think he's expecting to turn the corner at the house and see her alive and well, but he's not going to. He's not."

I shrugged. "He didn't seem too broken up about Trixie either."

"No," she said with a sniff, wiping tears from her cheek. "No, he didn't. I wish I knew what's wrong. I really wish I knew."

And so did I. More than anything I wanted inside James's head.

When I pulled into the driveway, Emily did not get out. She just sat there silently with the rectangular urn on her lap and cried.

"Will you be okay?" I asked.

She turned to me, those same tears in her eyes and said, "I don't know."

Once inside, she kicked off her shoes and slumped down on the couch with the urn still on her lap, just like in the car. She sat there and waited—for what, I had no idea. Waited for James to come to his senses, probably.

As I sat down beside her, not only did she look hurt and scared, her face betrayed a deep loneliness. "He's been this way ever since we got married," she said. "He was passionate while we were engaged, but now . . ." She sniffed and absently stroked the urn like Trixie was still sitting on her lap. "He's like a brick wall. Nothing can knock him down."

As I watched her, I could see only James's smile, nonchalant and carefree. He was probably passing the day at work like any other, completely oblivious to his wife's emotional plight, and his returning home would change nothing. Anger welled up inside me. I couldn't believe my best friend was mistreating his wife like this.

"Sorry I can't be of any more help," I told her.

She set Trixie's ashes on the end table and dried her tears with the back of her hand. "I don't think anyone can, really. This is one of those things I have to work out for myself." She shook her head and stared at the floor. "I'll be okay. I just want a decent shower and a nap."

I sought her eyes, but she did not look up at me. "I'm not going to leave until you promise me you'll be okay," I said.

When her eyes did meet me, they were red and watery. "I'll be fine," she said. "I swear."

"Go on then," I said. "I'll let myself out." My heart started beating like crazy, and I had no idea why at the time. As I think back now, I believe my subconscious was trying to warn me.

Emily said goodbye and disappeared into her bedroom.

I should have let myself out the moment she left the living room, but I didn't. That is the first thing I truly regret about all of this. I opened the front door loudly enough for her to hear it from down the hall and closed it with a bit of emphasis. On all fours, I hid behind the kitchen table, where I had a good view of the hallway leading to the bathroom.

Emily wandered into the bathroom. The door remained open,

spilling light into the otherwise dark hall. A metallic squeak started the hissing showerhead, and soon steam poured out of the open bathroom.

To this day, I do not know what possessed me. Before I knew it, I was softly padding down the blue shag carpet toward the bathroom. My approach masked by the shower, I stepped into the well-decorated washroom, complete with double sinks and a bathtub with a floral print shower curtain. Emily was humming a tune to herself, but I heard no joy in it.

Set in my decision, I took a bar of soap from the sink. I crawled to the back of the bathtub and stuck my hand behind the shower curtain just enough to slip the soap bar down into the tub. Without wasting another moment, I left the bathroom, fled down the hall, and went out the front door as silently as possible.

I felt absolutely horrible the whole way home. I knew I'd never be able to forgive myself if anything truly terrible happened to Emily, but I had to know. A man losing his dog is one thing; pets die all the time. But a man's wife getting rushed to the ER? That's something on a completely different level.

When the phone rang later on that night, my stomach twitched because I knew exactly who was calling and what he going to tell me. Only I was wrong. So, so wrong.

"Emily's dead," James said over the line.

Words turned to ash in my mouth. I probably stayed silent for a whole minute before I could work up the courage to ask him how such a thing had happened.

"She slipped on a bar of soap in the shower," he said impassively. "Cracked her skull on the bathtub faucet and bled out long before I came home."

Had he been anyone else, I would've heard sniffles and bawling from the other end.

"You want me to come over?" I asked him.

"If you want," he said. "Otherwise I'm probably just going to get some sleep."

After hanging up, I couldn't get Emily's face out of my head. I figured the way to a man's heart is through his wife, so I had only meant to try getting James to show a bit of sympathy for a sprained ankle or a concussion, not a lethal accident.

I didn't get a chance to see him again until the day of the viewing. He acted like nothing was abnormal when I met him at his house. He didn't choke up while I drove him to the funeral home. He didn't shed a single tear or even mention his late wife. I expected some measure of silence from a surviving husband, but his complete lack of conversation disturbed me.

Lingering by the casket was almost too much to bear. In it lay not just the wife of my best friend but the woman whose death was *my* fault. Still, James's secret remained buried beneath his unmovable exterior.

After the funeral the next day, James did not go home and cry himself to sleep; instead, he nestled in the corner of his couch and read a book. That night, I peeked into his bedroom window and saw him sleeping peacefully. Never once did he subconsciously reach over to hug his departed wife. He just lay on his side and slept as soundly as a baby. No guilt. No grief.

Emily became as quickly forgotten as his mother and Trixie were.

He called me up for drinks a few nights later. This was it, I thought. This would be the moment I had waited for.

We walked to B-Dubs and seated ourselves in a booth near the big, flat-screen TV. Even after a few beers, James said nothing about Emily between mouthfuls of pretzels and chicken wings. He only talked about the news or joined me in becoming absorbed with tonight's hockey match. For a few guiltless minutes, I even forgot he had been married at all.

Long enough was long enough, I decided. During the commercial break, I regarded James with all seriousness and took a swig from my Pilsner glass. "Do you miss Emily?" I asked him straight out.

He shrugged. "Of course I do. Why?"

"Because you're doing a damned good job of fooling me," I said. "I've not once seen you cry since your mother died. Surely your own *wife* could warrant some tears?"

"You forget I walk a different path than you," he said with a smile.

I stole one of his pretzels while he sank back into the game. "Then tell me about this path," I said.

"I can't. I already told you."

"Try me."

James shook his head. "You can't go off trying to find fate," he said. "Fate comes knocking on *your* door, and what it gives you is what it gives you."

"So fate entrusted you with the meaning of life?" I asked rhetorically. "And when *fate* killed your mother, your dog, and your wife, that gives you license to stop acting like a human being?" My brow darkened, and I slammed my glass down on the tabletop.

"Goddammit, that's not good enough," I said.

"What *is* good enough, then?" he said firmly. Not *angrily*. Firmly. "Until you stop trying to search, nothing will ever be good enough."

My anger flared up again, but before I could retort, the waitress wandered over and left our checks facedown on the table.

"I'll get that," said James, swooping up my check. "Money is the least of your worries right now."

I leaned back in my chair and felt to make sure the clumsy lump in my jacket pocket was still there. "I just don't get you anymore," I told him. "You don't care enough about your own wife to cry at her funeral, and here you are, picking up my check. Damn nice of you, if you ask me."

We walked back to his house. He didn't say a word, and neither did I. James was no longer the man I once knew better than most. Instead, I was walking alongside a complete stranger.

Both of us stepped into the front hallway. James shut the door and went to the hall tree to hang his jacket. For several long moments, his back was turned.

"Drop to your knees!" I shouted at him. "Hands behind your head!" The revolver wavered in my hands; I could not believe what I was doing. The wooden handgrip was already slick with sweat.

James sank to his knees, calm as a two-toed sloth. "Is this *really* necessary?" he asked with a roll of his eyes and a sigh.

"It is," I replied.

"What do you want?" he asked, as composed and phlegmatic as ever.

"I want to see you on your knees, pleading for your goddamned life," I said.

"Why?" he said with a shrug of his eyes.

"Because I'm going to kill you if you don't tell me your goddamned secret!"

James did not even stir. Any normal man would have pissed himself already. "I've told you before," he said, calmly. "I can't tell you."

"Like *hell* you can't." I pistol-whipped the base of his neck. He crumpled forward and rolled over on his back. Blood pooled, darkening the shag carpet. He winced and painfully lolled his head from side to side as I could smell the warm scent of his blood.

"Stop," he wheezed. His eyes, though pained, did not emit hatred, sorrow, fear, or confusion. "You don't know what you are doing . . ."

I knelt and straddled his torso. While keeping the gun trained on his face, I got right up in his face and shook him. "Then *tell* me what I'm doing!" I shouted at him. "Goddammit, tell me!"

James knocked the revolver from my hand, and it slid out of reach under the sofa. Instead of diving after the gun, I wrapped both hands around his throat and slowly constricted his windpipe.

His eyes radiated unmovable calm as they locked with mine. Hot, angry tears ran down my cheeks. "I didn't want to do this, Jimmy," I told him. "I didn't want it to end like this. Trixie and Emily—they were my fault. I wanted to get in your head, but you just didn't care!"

"I . . . *do* care . . ." he wheezed, fighting my iron grip. His face was growing drained and pale. "I have just . . . transcended . . . things . . . that have no bearing on the next world . . ."

I shook him hard. "How?! *Why*?!"

He stared at the ceiling with glazed, faraway eyes. His voice gurgled in his throat. "I have seen . . ."

"Seen *what*?"

James didn't blink. He stopped struggling. His strength vanished. The vitality in his clear eyes dimmed.

I hovered above his still body, mortified at what I had done. I began shaking uncontrollably. I had killed my best friend. My best friend! I had killed him for a secret that he'd taken to the grave.

I contemplated the gun under the sofa. I clenched it in both hands, stared down its cold, unfeeling barrel, the unyielding blackness that would await me. But after all I'd done, I couldn't bring myself to use it even if I'd bothered to load it.

That was when the epiphany struck me.

We all get one chance around this big, blue marble. Just one. When it comes to an end, that's it. And James knew that. He knew no amount of mourning could bring back his mother. He knew that rage alone never accomplished anything. So he simply sought to *live*. Come what may.

That's why I'm not angry about sitting here on death row for premeditated murder. It's what I deserve. And no amount of bitterness or anger can change that.

I don't need forgiveness. I don't want a prayer of absolution. I just want you to share this message with the rest of the world, to help make it a better place. You do that, and I guarantee James will live on forever.

THE UNDERBELLY

My first concrete childhood memory took place in a cellar, and since then every house I had lived in had included a basement. Somehow a home seemed incomplete without a cellar of some kind. Something about them felt earthy, primal, a convenient place to get away from the rushed pace of surface life.

The realtor led my wife, my two daughters, and I into darkness. Unlike the carpeted stairway leading to the Tudor-style house's second floor, these weathered planks creaked at every movement. Thick dust filled the air.

After nine steps, we touched down on the hard floor. The agent pulled the frayed string on a hanging bulb, and instantly the ambience transported me back to my boyhood, back to simple games of exploration in dusky corners.

Never in my life had I been in a cellar such as this. Walls of flagstone instead of cement. A sweet, musty smell as only a basement connoisseur could appreciate. Small cracks in the floor spidering out across the empty expanse. No windows peered out into the yard; only the single bulb illuminated our silent surroundings.

The girls loved the cellar despite its shadows, as did I. They had already set their little minds on exploring beyond the bulb's range before the real estate agent cautioned against it. "There aren't any more light fixtures down here," he said. "Probably not a good idea to venture off in the dark."

My wife couldn't stop smiling once we made our way back up the stairs into the kitchen. My fidgety daughters clasped their hands together in anticipation of romping in the backyard, exploring the forest, and beginning an archaeological dig in the far corner of the basement. The wife and I needed no further prompting to put in an offer.

I will go down on record as saying I didn't put much stock in ghost stories, yet some aspect of that basement both entranced and scared the holy hell out of me. A grownup knows there are no boogeymen under his bed, no monsters in his closet, no people living beneath the stairs. He tells his kids this and, for the most part, believes it himself. But every now and then, a grownup has to check under his own bed just to make sure.

My pessimistic side expected something dreadful to happen before our closing date. Any day a message could appear on our answering machine:

We're sorry, but the house inspection uncovered extensive water damage in the subflooring.

We're sorry, but the owners have decided to rescind the sale and take the house off the market.

We're sorry, but the whole house burned to the ground.

That call never came. My wife and I signed the escrow papers with the absent seller's agent, our realtor handed us the keys, and suddenly we were homeowners.

ठ ⅄ ଡ଼

The kids spent the first few days getting lost in the many rooms. When they asked if they could explore the basement, my immediate answer was no. In a house this old, there was no telling what kind of rusted nails or black widows lurked in the shadows.

"Daddy has to scare away all the monsters before you can play down there," I told them.

In all honesty, I did not intend to venture down into the previously unseen corner of my new house. However, the night we finished moving in, my wife asked if I would please investigate the cellar so the girls would stop pestering her.

This is how I ended up in the musty underbelly of our new home—alone.

My shoes echoed on the cement floor when I reached bottom, and a suffocating miasma of darkness enshrouded me. From the foot of the steps, I could see only the sharp outline of the door leading to the kitchen. Though I'd purposely left it open, it creaked in the breeze of the girls chasing each other past the breakfast bar. My line of light diminished with each pass.

I swallowed and fumbled my hands through the darkness. To turn on the dangling bulb, I had to tug on the light cord so hard I thought the moisture-stained string would snap.

For some reason, the basement seemed darker than it had the day the realtor showed the house. Something about it felt more closed, more claustrophobic than I had remembered. A wayward chill rattled its way down my spine. Cellars were usually colder than the rest of the house by virtue of being underground, but when had it ever been that cold in mid-summer?

There was, of course, nothing directly under the ladder-like stairs, though this did not keep me from looking. Nothing lurked in the far corner behind the steps either, yet I still checked just to make certain.

To distract myself from recalling old campfire stories, I entertained visions of where a pool table would fit. A foosball table over there. A dartboard on that wall. My wife's preserved fruits and jams on a shelf next to this wall.

The cellar was twice as big as expected. When I chanced around the corner from the light, beyond where the realtor had taken us, I had anticipated seeing the furnace, the water heater, and the laundry hookups. Instead, the room continued. The whole basement was an inverted *u* shape, with the kitchen steps at one tip of the *u*.

Unfortunately, the swaying light from the distant bulb extended no further than where I stood. Interminable blackness stretched before me.

At the third step from the bottom of the stairs, I called up into the kitchen, "Hon, I'm gonna need a flashlight."

She brought me down a steel-cased flashlight, an old hand-me-down from my grandfather kept mostly for its sentimental value, and then marched back upstairs. The flashlight bulb still lit when I flicked the hollow switch, but the innards couldn't squeeze as much juice out of D-cell batteries as a new flashlight would've.

From the stairs, I crept to the edge of the naked bulb's range. The flashlight did not pierce the darkness nearly as well as I'd hoped. It cast a wan yellow light on the cracked, dirty floor, illuminating a glassy circle only five or six inches in diameter.

At the bend, a broken shelf dangled from the wall, probably where the previous owner's wife had stored all of her jams and jellies. Beside it lay a few bent and broken nails, rusted all the way through. An old aluminum container of what smelled faintly of kerosene sat in the far corner beside a collection of musty planks of plywood and pegboard. The floor leveled off further down, leading to a circular storm drain that had corroded to an aged, chestnut color.

A soft, whooshing sound greeted me from behind. I whirled around, expecting to find my oldest daughter having snuck down the stairs to play a joke on me, but no one was there. I heaved a sigh laden with stress, and the windy noise came again, familiar this time. The claustrophobia had merely amplified the sound of my own breathing.

Even so, my pulse did not calm. Just as I turned the last corner in the basement, my surroundings plunged completely in darkness. The light bulb from around the bend was a distant memory, something from another lifetime.

I held my breath for a few moments. The sound came again.

Still holding my breath, I panned the small circle of light across the back wall. The masonry lay about ten feet distant. On my third full pan of the wall, the yellow beam settled on something much, much closer than ten feet away, something moist, black, and about the size of a golf ball.

It was an eye.

The pupil contracted in the light. A deep, guttural growl descended from beneath it. I jerked back with a muted scream as a muzzle full of yellow fangs snapped where my face had just been. The moist clomp of teeth and the rattling of iron came again in the same place.

My heart pounded in my chest. Stumbling backwards, I trained the trembling flashlight in the direction of the noise. Black and brown fur surrounded foaming teeth. Four canine paws padded around, nails clicking on the cement with each step. Clamped around all four ankles, thick iron manacles were chained to the cellar wall.

Each spasmodic snap of this coal black Doberman's jaws made my entire body flinch. The dog could no longer reach me where I stood, but the hot wind of rotten-meat breath and wet mongrel stench filled my nostrils. The entire cellar shook with every bark. Hate radiated in its eyes as the flashlight beam caught the reflective rods and cones.

More childhood memories sprang to life. Nearly losing my pinky to a friend's Rottweiler when I was five. Outrunning a pit bull down a country road when I was twelve. Watching a friend's kid sister get mauled by a cocker spaniel.

Fear does strange things to a person. Some, when confronted with their phobias, turn tail and run. Others wet themselves and curl up into a ball. Only a very select few stand eye to eye with their worst nightmares and let them have it.

Me? If I had a metal baseball bat, I would've bashed the damned thing's skull in. I would've claimed revenge against every large dog that had ever scared, threatened, or hurt anyone.

At least, I believed this for a span of five seconds before the jaws clapped shut with another wet and meaty clomp that shattered my resolve. Another moment later, I was yanking the pull cord at the base of the steps and racing back upstairs.

From the kitchen I could still hear it. The barking, the growling, the impatient clicking of canine fingernails. My wife, however, was emptying the boxes of kitchen utensils as though nothing was amiss.

"Do you hear that?" I asked her.

"Hear what?" she said.

I shook my head. "Never mind."

She looked up from the Tupperware collection and said, "So it is safe for the kids?"

I couldn't tell her about the Doberman. Knowing her, she'd have completely lost it. She would've checked herself and the kids into a hotel just to make sure they were safe. "I'll see about installing a few more light fixtures this weekend," I said. "Until then, I think it'd be best if we all stayed out of the basement. It's far too dark down there."

The next morning, I waited until she left for work and the kids went off to school. I called Animal Control, hid a key for them under the doormat, and drove to the office.

ד ג ע

Even leaving work early, somehow I knew something was wrong. I could smell it in the air. Not the crisp, clean scent of a spring afternoon but more like burning kerosene from a distant arsonist's fire. No one was home. No Animal Control vans had parked in the driveway.

Bad feelings ranked on my list with ghost stories. No point in getting worked up over possibilities.

Considering our mail had yet to start forwarding from our old address, I was surprised to see two items waiting for me in the mailbox. One turned out to be a handwritten notice from Animal Control left from their visit, the other a blank envelope bearing only my name in a hasty, arthritic scrawl. No address. No return address. No stamp.

"Dear Homeowner," said the Animal Control's postcard, "no animal matching the description you provided was found on or near the premises. If you require further assistance, please contact us at . . ."

I crumpled the cardstock in my fist. My instructions had been clear. How could they have misinterpreted "There is a Doberman chained in my basement"? How could they have not smelled its damp, foul stench or horrid breath?

In a huff, I ripped open the envelope. A single piece of cream-colored paper slid out into my palm. The script carried the same shaky, painful handwriting. No salutation, no signature.

It said in large, easy-to-read letters:

Do not let it out.
It will torment you, haunt you, but you cannot give in.
You MUST not.
Whatever you do, do not let it out.

Standing on the porch, I stared at the note for at least five minutes. Then I found myself staring at the house. No, not the house. What lay beneath the house. The underbelly.

I walked through the front door with firm, heavy steps. Not even bothering to drop my briefcase in the den, I went straight into the kitchen, down the rickety steps, and as far as the flashlight I'd left at the bottom of the stairs would take me.

Right before my tormentor.

The Doberman shied away from the beam for only a moment before its low growling resumed. It pounced. The short chains caught the dog in mid-leap and whiplashed it back to the concrete. The beast snarled, got to its feet, and pounced again. Every time it leaped and snapped, the stressed chain dislodged a few more chips of cracked cement from the wall.

How could Animal Control have missed this? How could they not have seen this ugly scar of black flesh marring my house?

In the dim flashlight beam, I reread the strange note. It was impossible for me to tell who had written it, but I had a roving suspicion.

ꝏ ꝏ ꝏ

From my mortgage documents, I gleaned the name of the previous owner. He'd been notably absent when we closed on the house—the seller's agent had taken care of all the paperwork—and I was beginning to understand why. A quick search of county records for any nearby property owned by this same gentleman turned up one solid hit.

Less than five minutes later, I was in my car, following the road to the address I'd scribbled on a note card. At a small ranch in the suburbs, no one answered my knock. The peephole darkened for a few seconds, and I could hear someone on the other side of the door.

My second knock was louder than the first. "Open up," I called through the door. "We need to talk."

No reply.

"I bought your house," I said.

Silence.

The deadbolt turned, and an older man in glasses, probably in his late sixties, peeked out from behind the brass door chain. His shifty eyes scanned me up and down before softening like he had just come from his granddaughter's funeral. He frowned, unhooked the chain, and gestured his chin in a grudging, wordless invitation.

Articles I could easily envision in a Tudor-style home—a grandfather clock, oil paintings with wooden frames, a cabinet filled with collectible plates—decorated the place. Unlike my house, his whole dwelling held an intimate, homely ambience. Not a single trace of dog scent or kerosene lingered in the air.

The old man sank into the living room recliner, and I claimed the couch opposite him. "I am sorry this had to happen to you, sir," he said, his head hung in shameful apology. "You seem like a good man. I can see it in your eyes."

"Have you always been in the habit of chaining vicious dogs in your basement?" I asked.

"I don't have a basement anymore," he replied.

"So you thought it'd be funny to hide a starving Doberman in my house?" I snapped.

"A Doberman, you say?" The old man's eyes creased with a deeper frown. When he looked at me, his entire frame shuddered with untold age. "For me, it was a Rottweiler. For my departed wife, it was a greyhound. My grandchildren saw a toy poodle, but my two sons couldn't see it at all."

Had I met this man before buying the house, I'd have thought him a bit too lost in the hedge maze. As it was, I almost began to believe him.

"All it takes is the right person to contain it," he said. "I'm just not strong enough anymore. Keeping that house would have endangered everything I hold dear."

"Honestly," I said, "I don't give a damn whether you chained anything in my basement or not. All I care about is getting it out of my house." I thrust the note under his nose. "I take it this is your doing?"

The old man did not even so much as glance at the scrawled message. "Listen to me carefully," he said, pushing the note aside. "It will gnaw into your brain, make you do things you never thought you would do. But whatever you do, *whatever* you do, *don't let it out.*"

Choking back a startled cough, I said, "Excuse me? It's just a stupid dog, isn't it?"

"*Just* a dog?" he replied, eyebrows arched as high as they could go. "You came all this way to see me, and you *still* think it's 'just a dog'?" His eyes narrowed, and he shook a gnarled finger at me. "You know what it is far better than you think. I do not know all its secrets, but I do know this: it wants out, and it will do anything—and I mean *anything*—to escape. I have seen it try to trick some people into thinking it is sweet and cuddly. Others it frightens into setting it loose. Unless I miss my guess, sir, you have had a history with large, violent dogs, as I have."

I began shifting uncomfortably in my seat. How could he have known? And what was he implying?

"Board it up," he instructed. "Lay down cinder blocks and mortar or fill the whole basement with cement and seal that abomination away for all time."

"I can't just go home and fill my basement with cement," I said.

"Then you have my sympathies," he said. "Good luck."

He then ushered me out the door before I thought to ask why he never filled the basement with cement himself.

No matter how many times I rang his doorbell or knocked on his door, the old man refused to answer. At home I called the number I'd found from county records and left a message. The next morning this number was no longer in service. A casual drive by his house revealed a SOLD sign tacked in the front lawn.

♂ � ⍾

The rest of the day, I did not even acknowledge the stairs leading out of the kitchen. I just couldn't figure out how to deal with that . . . *thing*. My official word to the wife was that I'd need to thoroughly clean out the basement before the girls could play down there. I trotted out every basement hazard I could think of to drive my case home—rusted nails, splintered boards, brown recluses—and the matter was dropped.

That night, I could not sleep. Something woke me every time REM sleep threatened to kick in. My eyes would shoot open, and in the dark I would lie there and listen over my heartbeat until weariness dragged me back to sleep. The third time, I remained alert for a bit longer. The sound came again, more distinct this time: a distant bark that seemed to shake the walls.

Certain it would wake the kids, I stepped into the hallway to gauge the volume. However, the moment I left my room, the noise stopped. Shaking my head, I returned to bed only to be awakened moments later by the barking's return.

And what was that *smell?* Gasoline?

Behind closed eyes I envisioned burning down the whole house just to get rid of that damned thing. However, something far less extreme would suffice. As I made my way down to the garage, the distant snarling seemed to resonate directly into my brain, rattling my every thought. From the tool bench, I grabbed a sledgehammer and crept back into the kitchen. The barking had grown louder, more vengeful. How could this have not roused the kids? While standing at the foot of the stairs, I cringed at each successive bark, each more nerve-wracking than before. Vindictive canines tended to bark in a steady rhythm; this one somehow seemed to explode at the exact moment I gathered up my confidence, somehow seeing into my thoughts.

For several agonizing moments, I stared down the descending steps. All was darkness. That strange smell, the brain-whirling tang of stagnant kerosene, wafted up from Hell. Then, one dusty step at a time, I descended into my own nightmare.

At the bottom of the stairs, I tugged on the light cord. The darkness remained. When I yanked a second time, the bulb flashed for an instant, and the old string snapped off from the light fixture. I stumbled forward in the darkness and felt around for the flashlight I'd left at the foot of the stairs.

The barking intensified and reverberated through the hollowness of the cellar. It magnified like the concussion wave of a grenade. My brain reeled from the noise and the kerosene scent and threatened to crawl down my spinal cord to escape its anguish.

Leaning the sledgehammer against the wall, I clicked on the flashlight. For the longest time, we stared at each other—it in hatred, I in revulsion and dread. Its damnable eyes reflected the violent passion of every contemptible canine I had ever encountered. I imagined my own severed pinky in the mouth of the Rottweiler, my gouged-out eye impaled between pit bull teeth. I saw a chunk of my friend's sister's upper lip in the fangs of the cocker spaniel, my youngest daughter's neck crushed between this Doberman's jaws.

Exchanging the lit flashlight for the leaning sledgehammer, I paced in front of the monster. Not once did I turn my eyes from the creature's coal black fur, its rising hackles, its glowering stare. This thing had invaded my house, my fond childhood memories. This thing had governed my every thought since the day I signed on the x.

From high above my head, I swung the sledge down on the unsuspecting Doberman's head with a wet, thudding crack. The blow traveled all the way down my arms and stabbed pain through my shoulders. Without even a whimper, the dog collapsed. A gaping hole in its skull gushed crimson onto the cement. Blood trickled into the floor cracks, creating rivers like an atlas. The heady incense of lantern fuel heightened from the undisturbed kerosene container.

Behind bleary eyes, I chuckled. The deed had been done, but I wanted more. I wanted revenge for every person who had been frightened, bitten, or mauled by any kind of feral canine. Instead of walking away, I smashed its brains with the hammer again and again and again, until the evil thing's skull was unrecognizable. Then I dropped the bloody sledgehammer's head onto the cement with a heavy, metallic thud and let the haft fall back against the wall.

Satisfied, I unclasped the manacles chaining the dog to the wall. From the kitchen I retrieved three large garbage bags, bagged them inside each other for added strength, and undertook the gruesome task of shoving the carcass into them. The closer I came to its diseased hide, the more my eyes watered, as though the dog had bathed in gasoline and expired meat. Closing off the drawstrings did little to cut off the odor.

Inch by inch, I dragged the bag up the basement steps and down our long, winding driveway before tossing it on the curb for the garbage collectors.

That night, I slept better than I had ever remembered.

♂ ♈ ♋

I awoke in the ER.

The police detective who visited me said my wife and daughters hadn't survived the fire.

"Coroner said they went in their sleep," he said after delivering the news. "Carbon monoxide poisoning took them before the fire burned out of control."

For the longest time, I could not breathe, as though someone had struck me square in the solar plexus with a baseball bat. My eyes bulged with tears. No words came; nothing I could say could alter the reality I had already known to exist.

"Sir," said the detective, "were you aware that we found traces of kerosene in the remains of your home?"

My head shook.

"Do you understand what this implies?" he asked.

My head hung in shame. What had indeed happened that night? Would I ever know?

"You are under arrest for arson," the detective said. "You have the right to remain silent. Anything you say or do may be used against you in a court of law. Do you understand?"

ಶ ℣ ಖ

From the witness stand, I told the court my story. I told them about the Doberman, the old man, the inexplicable fire. No one believed me, but the prosecution could not establish a plausible motive for me to burn down my own house. My family was well off, and character witnesses established that my marriage was solid and I loved my kids unconditionally. But that wasn't enough to convince the jury of my innocence.

Sometimes, I think they may be right.

I still see it in my dreams—the eye, the teeth. Sometimes I can even smell it, that rotten meat stench mixed with lantern fuel. Sometimes I dream that I am in the underbelly of my house, dousing the brain-smattered corpse with kerosene, igniting it with a struck match. Sometimes I watch myself throwing kerosene on all of our furniture, on my sleeping wife and daughters, even on myself.

About a month after my conviction, the old man who had once owned the house came by out of the blue to visit me at the penitentiary. Through the Plexiglas, through the black visitor's phone, he said, "You let it out. I *told* you not to let it out."

"But I didn't let it out," I told him. "I killed it. I took care of it."

"Is death not a release?" His brow creased, and he shook his head like a disapproving grandfather. "You only made it stronger, and I see it has already rewarded you for your service." Then he turned to leave.

"Wait!" I called out after him. My heart thudded in my chest so hard I could barely hear anything else. He *knew* things he couldn't possibly know, and he was the only one who could vouch for my innocence. "Did I—did I really do it? Did I really kill them?"

He faced me, his bespectacled blue eyes radiating both surprise and satisfaction. For a single instant, I saw the crazed, starved look of that Doberman reflected in his lenses, and I backed away from the Plexiglas.

"Whether you killed them or not is immaterial," he said. "Now you must live with what you have done. I only hope its next victim is stronger than you were."

I stood there in mute silence as I watched him go.

SOLD

Waiting on the driveway at the yard sale, Gerald wanted a quarter more than anything. Shiny, tarnished, or even bent—he didn't care what state the coin came in. Some of the world's greatest treasures could be bought with a quarter. Gumballs. Sticky hands. Butterfly rings. Plastic spacemen. All of these and more could be purchased with twenty-five cents, yet not even two pennies jangled together in his pocket. At that moment, a whole quarter amounted to a small fortune in his eight-year-old eyes.

He stood next to his grandmother and greedily eyed the box of odds and ends sitting on the last table in the summer grass. *"WHOLE BOX, 25¢,"* the hand-scribbled note proclaimed. At such a price, Gerald did not care what it contained. He could have scored plastic army men, magnetic board games, decks of dog-eared playing cards with interesting pictures on the backs. Such a large box was bound to hold something he could occupy himself with for an afternoon, but the mystery was far more important than the actual contents.

Wishes didn't fill his pockets any faster. They were still empty—except for a few rolls of lint he kept picking at.

His grandmother selected a flowery sundress from a pile of clothes on the neighboring table and chatted with the woman in charge of the sale. This being the third yard sale his gran had taken him to that afternoon, Gerald quickly grew bored and milled about, focusing on the box all the while. Faded, outdated clothes covered one of the three folding tables arranged in a *u*. Old garden tools and yellowed Tupperware containers hid another table. His coveted box sat on the third table amid a collection of old, broken toys, some of which he already had at home.

With his arms crossed, Gerald sighed and waited for his gran to finish with boring clothes. All he wanted was a quarter, a single, lousy quarter, and she could drag him along to yard sales for the rest of the day if she wanted.

She paid seventy-five cents—three whole quarters!—for some clothes, tucked the shirts and dresses under her arm, and smiled in her sunglasses and wicker hat.

"Ready to go, Gerry?" she said to him while he grimaced against the hot sun.

His faced scrunched into a desperate plea. He did not say anything at first, only let her guess at what bothered him. And maybe he would get a sympathy quarter out of the ordeal. After all, if she had spent three quarters here and more than a dollar at the other two yard sales, it stood to reason she had more.

"What's wrong, Gerald?"

"Can I have a quarter, Gramma?" he said timidly, even though he had wanted to throw a tantrum instead. He had learned long ago that a pitiful request worked worlds more than whining and crying.

Her sunglasses smiled again, and she stooped closer to his eye level. "Seen something that tickles your fancy, eh?"

He nodded. "Can I have a quarter, please? I . . . can clean the dishes when we get back."

"Well, bless your dear heart. You don't need to do that." She opened her change purse and clinked through not one, not two, but more than a *dozen* quarters. Gerald's eyes widened. Oh, the gumballs and space aliens he could buy with that much money! "Make sure you purchase wisely," she said. "You wouldn't want to buy a toy some poor child's mother put up for sale by mistake, now would you?"

Gerald didn't see any other kids playing in the yard or hanging around the lady running the sale. He just wanted the box. "I will," he said.

"Then here you go." She smiled and gave him not one, but *two* quarters. "This is for being such a good boy today."

Overjoyed beyond words, Gerald skipped up to the table where the box sat. He held one of his shining coins in the air like it was a hard-won trophy. And certainly it was for him: he had sweated through three yard sales to earn this.

"And what can I get for you, young man?" asked the sales lady.

Gerald smiled like the summer sun shined on him alone. "I've got a quarter for that box on the end there," he said. He thrust the quarter at her as though someone else might steal his prize before he could complete the sale.

Her smile faded somewhat, but she took the worn coin and dropped it in the cashbox with a plunk. "It is all yours," she said.

With rapture he ran two steps to his box and lugged it off the table with both hands. His grandmother could have easily carried the box under one arm, but to him, it was huge. He summoned all his eight-year-old strength to hoist the box into his arms and lifted a knee to boost it into a better grasp. The height of the box kept him from seeing its entire contents as he craned his neck over the top flap, yet he could see various odd and ends—old dolls with dirt smudges, antiquated wooden clothespins without a spring hinge, miscellaneous game pieces made out of wood instead of plastic.

The junk he would keep. The dolls he'd probably throw out or give to Billy's bulldog.

Gerald thought about what his grandmother had said, and he wondered whose these had been before he bought them. "Did any of this belong to your kids?"

A tear wet her eyes. "My . . . daughter went away a long time ago," she said. "My son is in university."

Gerald was not entirely sure what "university" was, but he put on his most sincere grin. "Then," he said, heaving the heavy box again with a helpful knee, "I will take good care of them."

He did not, of course, mention his plan for the dolls.

"Thank you," said the lady, wiping the corner of her eye with a blouse sleeve.

The other quarter he spent more selflessly. After setting his box down at his feet, he bought an old, hand-me-down action figure that he already had, intending to give it to Billy, who didn't have one. Then he went back over to his waiting grandmother.

"I see you've found something," she said. "A *big* something, from the looks of it."

Gerald could think of nothing more than dumping out the whole box in his bedroom and spending the rest of the hot afternoon in air conditioning while sorting the contents of his find. His eyebrows rose "Can we go home now, Gramma?" he said, fighting for a better hold on his prize.

"Not yet." She answered as nicely as possible, but Gerald wanted to hear none of it. "We've one more yard sale, and then we can go home, okay?"

The boy frowned and got in the car. His mom and grandmother were always carting him around places, and he never had any say in the matter. So, with a sigh, Gerald crossed his arms and reclined beside his box in the back seat.

At the next garage sale, he just wanted to stay in the car. Having already found his treasure trove for the day, he doubted his gran would give him another quarter anyway. This idea lasted only a few minutes because the summer sun baked the car from the inside out until Gerald could stand it no longer. He got out of the car only to spend the next forever following his grandmother through the endless tables full of forgotten odds and ends.

But all the while he kept looking back to the car to make sure his find was still safe. After all, any old burglar could come up, smash the car window, and haul his box of loot away, never to be seen again. He would've chased the guy down if it came to that, so he watched his grandmother's car like it was Fort Knox itself.

Finally, his patience paid off. With a few items in an old paper grocery bag, his grandmother announced that she was ready to go home. And it was about time. Gerald had been ready to go home a long time ago, but he didn't say so because he was afraid of getting a whipping from his mother for sassing his dear grandmother.

The drive home dragged on even though home lay only a few blocks away. Gerald's every thought focused on the box and what he might discover deep within its contents. He imagined finding almost anything—a chunk of iron pyrite, a few magnets, an ancient Incan artifact, a dinosaur bone—and the more he dwelled upon the idea, the more he could not wait.

As soon as his grandmother parked in their driveway, Gerald vacated the car with his precious cargo. Before she could even get out the key to the front door, he stood on the front porch waiting for her. The moment she unlocked the door, Gerald shoved it open with his box and ran upstairs to his room.

Even though the air conditioning provided relief from the sweaty outdoors, Gerald barely noticed it. He burst into his room, closed the door, and overturned the box as quickly as he could. To his utter delight, hundreds of various doodads littered the carpet by his bedside.

He did not find an Incan artifact or a dinosaur bone of any kind, but he found many other things he believed were just as valuable: large paper clips, thumbtacks, metal washers, a rather heavy paperweight, some old action figures with missing thumbs, plastic dolls in fabric dresses, half an alphabet block set, bent 3x5" note cards, and a thousand other assorted things. He set the action figures aside; Billy would probably want to play with them later. The half-dozen dolls he was still not entirely sure what to do with. They seemed almost too nice to give to Billy's bulldog but too prissy not to destroy with firecrackers. In the end, he decided Billy would probably have a better idea of what to do with them than he did.

Then he started surveying and sorting the mess. Next to his bed he took stock of the ten yellowed alphabet blocks, the kind with a different letter on each side, and wondered what he could spell with them. But before he could pick one up, he studied the haphazard pattern they had already made. Being in the first grade, Gerald could read, but not as well as his grandmother could.

He recited the letters aloud to himself: "D-I-R-T-Y-T-H-I-E-F."

Then he recoiled. Blocks falling out of a box never spelled anything, and even if they did, it was by accident.

Still, the sight of the finger-pointing words sent a chill through his bones. Just so he would feel better, he shifted his eyes from the blocks and rolled them aside so they would spell something nonsensical. Only after that was done did his stomach stop fluttering enough for him to go back to enjoying his archaeology.

Metal things he put in one pile. Plastic things he put in another. Stripping the dolls of their dresses, he created a pile for fabric. Then he started a collection for wooden things. This forced him to look at the blocks long enough to round them up.

This time the ten blocks spelled *N-A-U-G-H-T-Y-B-O-Y*.

Gerald felt so afraid and angry at the same time that he stood and kicked half of them across the room. He stood panting and chanced a look at the blocks he could still see.

M-E-A-N-I-E.

Fighting down a scream, he ran to his blue-curtained window, undid the clasps, and shoved the window open with all his might. Without looking at the blocks, he gathered them one by one and threw them all out into the open air. They landed with a thud in his grandmother's flower garden, where, he assumed with satisfaction, they would eventually rot or be buried and forgotten in the rich topsoil.

A sigh escaped him. Satisfied his fright was over, he closed and latched the window and returned to his excavation site.

The moment he sat down amidst the mess, the doorbell rang. Probably his mother coming home by carpool, having forgotten her keys on the dining room table. Or maybe it was Billy, he thought. While sorting, he hoped it was Billy; those dolls would not destroy themselves.

Gerald heard his grandmother answer the door and waited for her to shout upstairs for him.

"Gerry!" she called, right on cue. "One of your little friends is here!"

But Gerald did not want to go downstairs. He was too busy sorting his treasures. "I'm up in my room, Gramma," he called back.

A little patter of steps jaunted up the carpeted staircase. As his bedroom door opened slowly, he heard those same small feet step inside.

"Hey, Billy," he said without looking up from his work.

His friend did not respond.

When Gerald looked up, his entire body shook. It wasn't Billy. It wasn't even a boy.

A girl of about eight stared straight through him. Her cheeks were sunken and sallow. Dark moons hung under her eyes like she had not slept in weeks. If he hadn't known better, he would say she looked dead. Barefoot, she wore a white dress that looked like it had been made out of the same material as the old dolls' dresses, a synthetic satin with lace that had been smudged from dirt and age.

The more Gerald looked at her eyes, the more he saw the eyes of a doll. The glassy finish, the overly large pupils, the anchored, plastic eyelashes. That deadened stare. Without even saying a word, she scared him more than anything he had ever seen on nighttime television.

"Where are my dolls?" she said.

He swallowed. "A—are these yours?" he managed to say, pointing to the pile of dolls and their dirty dresses.

"You bought my dolls?"

Gerald had no idea what to say. He never knew quite what to say to girls, especially those who were upset with him. "I bought them at a yard sale for a quarter," he said finally.

At that moment, the girl looked more like a doll than ever before. Her skin turned smooth and waxy, more peach colored than real flesh. Her toes fused together like a single, hollow piece of molded plastic. Her fingers stiffened into odd, doll-like positions.

"Two can play at this game," she said. "You can have my dolls if you want them, but I require something in return."

The girl smiled and vanished right before his eyes.

Pale as a sheet, Gerald ran downstairs to tell his gran, but as soon as he left his room, he noticed something was wrong.

The coat tree with his mother's jacket was missing. Emptiness stood where the planters right inside the door had once been. Foreign paintings covered the normally bare walls, and a line of shoes he did not recognize sat next to the hall closet.

Gerald broke into an urgent sprint back up to his bedroom.

A treadmill had taken over the spot where his bed used to be. Racks of dumbbells sat in place of his bookshelves. The carpet was a different color.

A man he had never seen before stormed into the room. "Hey!" he shouted, red-faced. "What the hell are you doing here?"

Mortified, Gerald stepped away from the man. Where was his mother, his grandmother? What was this man doing in his house? Gerald's eyes watered.

In the middle of the room, he saw four wooden blocks.

S-O-L-D, they spelled.

The scream caught in his throat, he ran past the stranger and out the front door. Instead of Gran's car, a candy-red convertible was parked in the driveway.

The angry man chased him out to the curb, but Gerald had already rolled up into a ball, sobbing his little heart out. Soon flashing squad cars pulled into the neighborhood, and the policemen asked him all kinds of questions.

They had no record of his mother or his gran on file. All the police could do was drive him down to the station until a social worker from Children's Services could come and claim him.

As Gerald stared through the car window and tearfully glimpsed his bedroom window for the last time, he wished beyond all wishing that his missing grandmother had been stingier with her quarters.

 strong ᚦ ᚤ ᚨ

Gerald passed from foster home to foster home for seemingly no reason at all. On any given day, he might come home from school—always a new school for each new foster home—and his foster parents would tell him they were sending him back to Children's Services to match him up with "a more suitable family." After the first few transfers, he started to notice a pattern: his foster parents would start acting weird for several days, and then he'd come home to the news.

His sixth or seventh foster family—he'd since lost track—had been tiptoeing around him lately, hardly ever looking him in the eyes and speaking to him only when necessary, and he knew exactly what was coming.

Over the next week, Gerald started saving up his allowance, one quarter at a time, in order to prepare for the worst. Some fosters were nice and would get him anything he needed—one even had a stack of *brand-spanking-new* comic books waiting for him on his first day!—but others had trouble remembering to buy him simple things like pencils or notebook paper, and he'd have to fend for himself and buy them from the school bookstore. So any time he saw a cast-off object at school—a lonely pencil half-hidden in the hall at school, a pink eraser broken in half, a mostly empty ballpoint pen—he would pick it up and add it to his collection, just in case.

After he'd saved a few dollars worth of allowance, Gerald was on the playground after school, waiting for the bus to arrive. He was scribbling doodles in a Gregg-ruled notepad with the most recent chewed-up, half-sharpened pencil he'd found, and after the lead broke for the hundredth time, he stared at the pencil instead of sharpening it, wondering for a moment whose it had been before he found it.

Wondered whether something worthless like this might ever find its way into a yard sale box marked "25¢."

He gripped the pencil so hard he felt it might break, but it didn't. He studied the artful pattern of teeth marks—not his own—along the yellow-painted length, the way the pink eraser had been torn off at so deep an angle that the metal ring tore through paper if he tried to erase anything, then he closed his eyes and pictured the hallway where he'd found it.

A few days ago, his classmates were chatting on the way to lunch, and he suddenly found himself thinking about Clay Aberdeen, a kid he knew but didn't really talk to that much. He found himself thinking about Clay trying to slide the pencil in his back pocket. Instead, the pencil clattered to the floor and rolled out nearly of sight, where it had rested until Gerald had picked it up.

On the playground, Gerald stood up and caught Clay about to hop on his bus. "Is this yours?" he said, thrusting the pencil at him. "I think you dropped it in the hallway."

Clay studied it for a second before a flash of recognition lit his face. "Hey, this was my favorite pencil," he said. "Always wondered what had happened to this. Thanks, Gerry."

Gerald spent the bus ride home trying to figure out exactly what had happened. There was no way he could have *guessed* the pencil was Clay's, of all people. The pencil had—well, it must've *spoken* to him somehow.

After rummaging through his backpack, he found a pink rubber eraser that was snapped in half, with "*TT'S*" written on it in blue pen. No idea where the other half had gone to or what the rest of the word was supposed to be. He held onto it just like he had done with the pencil, and he imagined a distraught Betty Barnes watching one of the fourth graders flexing the eraser into an arch, taunting her with it.

BETTY'S, the eraser had across its stretched surface.

Give it back! Gerald imagined her yelling. This only egged the boy on.

When the pink eraser suddenly split down the middle like an overcooked hot dog, Gerald felt like someone had snapped a wet towel against the small of his back. He sat up straight. The eraser fell from his fingers and tumbled down to the bus floor, where he quickly snatched it back up.

The next morning, he left the eraser on the corner of Betty's desk before she came in to class. Later on, he saw her showing the eraser to Becca and Lucy, and he overheard her talking about the kid who had broken it in half and tossed it out onto the playground.

But Gerald knew it was impossible for him to have known about any of that. A lucky guess, just like with Clay's pencil.

For the next several days, he saw every abandoned object with different eyes. A lost action figure discovered under the merry-go-round, a small spiral notebook left near the coat racks, a mostly empty handbag forgotten beneath a bush at the neighborhood park—he wondered whose they were and whether their original owners missed them. At first, he was afraid to touch the objects, for he could only imagine what kinds of things he would see.

But lost items, he decided, were meant to be found.

☞ ⅄ ⊘

His foster parents finally dropped the hammer at dinner. All the typical excuses spilled out of their mouths, and after hearing the usual "we're just not the right fit for you," Gerald tuned them out and stopped listening until they told him the case worker would come pick him up tomorrow evening after school.

He went upstairs and closed his bedroom door. Even though no one could see him, he'd sworn he would not cry, but the vow didn't last. He bawled into his pillow. He didn't really care that his fosters had had enough of their trial run. He just missed his family. His *real* family. Without any photographs, he could only summon mental pictures of his mom and dad and gran, and even those were beginning to fade with time.

Once the tears dried enough for him to see straight, he rummaged through his knapsack and pulled out the toy he'd found on the playground. This scuffed-up action figure—a representation of a minor character from some cartoon that wasn't on any more—it must've bounced and rolled under the merry-go-round a long time ago. Since the gap between the merry-go-round and the ground was too shallow to climb beneath, he'd only noticed it because he was lying facedown on the merry-go-round one day and had let his head dangle over the edge while he held onto the metal poles. A glance into the hidden world beneath the merry-go-round revealed a strange silhouette that he had needed a long tree branch to retrieve.

On his bed, he held the toy in both hands and closed his eyes. He was back on the playground, and soccer team captain Victor Jessup was tossing the toy back and forth between both hands. Francis Porter—who insisted everyone call him "Frank"—was reaching up to snatch the figure from Vic, but Vic was too tall and Frank too slow. Vic tossed the toy over to Clay, who tossed it over to Dylan Sherman when Frank got too close, and so on, until it came back to Vic.

"This guy's dumb and so's that stupid show," Vic said, shaking the toy just out of reach. "If you want this back so badly, *Francy*, then go find it." He dropped the action figure and kicked it across the playground like it was a soccer ball. None of the boys saw where it landed, but Gerald knew. He followed Frank's treasure as it sailed past the swings, bounced low across the grass and dirt, and landed in the hard-to-reach darkness beneath the spinning wheel of doom.

Gerald set down the action figure and picked up the purse he'd found in the park on his walk home from the bus stop. He gave a yelp upon witnessing a young woman standing in his room, the purse tucked under her arm. She was walking along when another figure—a man dressed in dark clothing—dashed up to her and tried ripping the handbag from her arm. The pair struggled for a moment, but the thief won out and took off to somewhere beyond the walls of Gerald's bedroom. The woman collapsed to her knees and began sobbing uncontrollably.

And then, just like the ghostly doll-girl who had banished him to this nightmare, this woman also vanished. It seemed he didn't even need to close his eyes anymore for the objects to tell him their stories.

He dug into the purse and found a worn wallet tucked inside—

empty except for some photographs of babies and mothers and grandparents. The faces of strangers made Gerald wish he still had photographs of his own family. As he leafed through the pictures, the robbed woman reappeared in his room. She was standing on the porch of a one-story house and hugged the elderly woman in one of the photographs. The house had garish, mint green siding.

Gerald would've recognized this house anywhere. It wasn't far from the park, and he often rode his bike by it.

The next morning, he gathered up all his meager allowance and left early for the bus without saying goodbye to his foster mother. He biked over to the ugly green house, set the handbag on the doorstep, rang the doorbell, and pedaled down the street before anyone could answer.

At school, he caught Frank in the hallway. "Didn't you lose this a while ago?" he said and handed him the action figure.

Frank's eyes looked about to burst. "I—I . . ."

"You're welcome," Gerald said with a wry smile. "And next time Vic calls you 'Francy,' call him 'Victoria,' okay?"

The rest of the day passed in a blur because he didn't want to remember it. He didn't say goodbye to any of his classmates because he hadn't the heart to tell them why. In all honesty, he didn't quite know why either. He'd been adrift ever since the yard sale, moving from foster home to foster home, from school district to school district. And he'd had enough.

After school, Gerald walked three blocks to the bus station instead of taking the school bus home. He tossed his two quarters into the receptacle and stared out his window until the bus passed through his old neighborhood.

On the outside, his parents' house had changed a little since the incident. The new owners had trimmed the bushes, put in a few new trees, and repainted the siding, but the blue curtain in the window of Gerald's bedroom remained the same. As did the untended garden right below it.

Careful to avoid the windows, Gerald approached the garden and fell to his hands and knees. He started digging with his fingers, not caring how much of a mess he made. They had to be here, he kept telling himself.

His fingernails struck something hard beneath the old topsoil. From the dirt he pulled out a single wooden alphabet block stained by dirt and age. The letters a, g, k, m, r, and u displayed in solid colors on its six sides. A smile on his face, he went right on digging and did not stop until he found three more blocks.

If the blocks were still here, that meant the dolls and everything else from the yard sale box had to be around also. Somewhere up in his old bedroom.

The *dolls*.

This had all started with the dolls.

As he rose from his knees, Gerald glanced at the four alphabet blocks he'd thrown into the grass.

G-I-F-T, they said.

He rang the doorbell, and a confused woman answered.

"I used to live here," he said. "When we moved, I think a box of my things got left behind."

"Well," she said, "now that you mention it . . . Hold on a moment." Gerald milled about on the porch until the lady brought a box of junk, the instantly recognizable "*WHOLE BOX, 25¢*" scrawled on its side. "Found this upstairs when we moved in. I always meant to donate or pitch it but never did."

Even from the top of the box he spied the dirty satin of a doll's dress. Gerald's heart leapt. He thanked the lady and sat out on the curb with the box of lost treasures.

He gingerly rummaged through the box until he found the largest doll and picked it up, holding it in both hands. He couldn't see anything special about it other than it looked almost exactly like the ghostly little girl who'd first appeared to him what felt like years ago. He stared right into the doll's weighted, plastic eyes—fell into them, *through* them—until he found himself somewhere else. He was inside a paperboard box, staring through a clear plastic window at other shelves filled with countless toys in colorful boxes. A toy store aisle.

A young girl of about three or four had the box tucked under her arm. Gerald—the doll—followed the girl everywhere. At bedtime, at playtime, or at meals, the girl kept her prized possession somewhere close at hand, if not in her lap or cradled beneath her arm.

Time passed in a blur, and the next thing Gerald knew he heard a steady beeping. He was tucked under the girl's arm again, just like always, only this time a small vinyl tube connected to the back of the hand holding him—the doll—close. Her grip was strong at first, so strong she would have choked him had he not been made out of molded plastic. And then the strength lessened each day just a little bit more, until the girl's hand went slack.

The beeping mutated into a solid, shrill tone that never ended. Gerald—the doll—found himself thrown over the side of the bed onto the floor to witness only the shuffling of countless shoes, one of which accidentally kicked him across the room.

Then, silence. Sobbing. Darkness. Next thing he knew, the woman from the yard sale was picking him up in the darkness and staring right at him. Tears obscured her eyes. And then she hugged him.

Years passed. Gerald found himself moved from a purse to a dresser top, from a dresser to a closet, from a closet to a box. Then, finally, open sky lightened the darkness. Blazing summer sun. He saw the interior of a car. The ceiling of a house.

And then Gerald's plastic eyes stared up at himself hovering above the box like a giant.

I should take these over to Billy's tomorrow, he heard his colossal self think. *He's still got some firecrackers left over from Fourth of July, right?*

All of a sudden, Gerald felt sick to his stomach. What had he done?

And then the girl—the doll's original owner—appeared in the room. Gerald felt the weights in his plastic eyes when he blinked at her. He felt the hairbrush-bristle eyelashes grazing his cheeks.

When he opened his eyes, he was sitting in his own room and staring down at the doll in his hands. The girl was standing right next to him, looking less and less like her favorite doll as the moments passed.

"I'm—I'm sorry," he said.

"Now you know what it feels like to be lost and forgotten," the girl said. "You have a gift. You should use it."

"I already have, I think," he said, looking back at the doll. "Here. This belongs to you."

The girl smiled with a touch of sadness. "You keep it. I don't need it anymore."

And then she disappeared, just like before.

Doll still in hand, Gerald ran downstairs and nearly collided with his grandmother on the landing.

"Careful!" she said with a big smile. "Now go wash up. Dinner's almost ready."

Gerald nearly broke out in tears as he hugged her. Everything was back in its place. Everything was as it should be. But then he looked down at the doll and knew that wasn't true at all.

Every lost object had a special, unique history, and somewhere out there, objects and their owners had been parted, either by time, distance, or even death. Everything had a story to tell, and it was up to him to find those stories.

♂ ⅄ ◑

For the rest of the summer, Gerald saved up every quarter of his allowance and was more than ready for his grandmother's final round of yard sales before school started up again. This time, he wasn't bored in the slightest. This time he picked up every item on display and sifted through every box and every bag in search of something that spoke to him when he touched it. Most things hadn't been cherished enough to leave a story only he could read, but every once in a while, he came across wonderful stories in even the most unremarkable objects. Things that spoke to him wanted for a good home; these items he promptly paid for with his hard-earned quarters. Others longed for their original owner, so he would tell the person manning the cashbox that he believed the item had been mistakenly put up for sale.

Summer ended. School started.

Everywhere Gerald went across the school grounds, he came across discarded items. Never again did he look down and disregard a watermelon-shaped gummy eraser half-buried in pencil shavings. A bent baseball card left under the bleachers. An action figure's green plastic gun sticking out of the playground mulch.

Each one of these he would scoop up and put in his knapsack, right next to the worn doll. By the end of the day, only the doll would remain.

And then he would head home, the young girl standing beside him while he waited for the bus.

WOLF HUNT

Article in the paper a few days ago reported increased wolf activity near the Omaha reservation, so I wasn't too surprised by the pack I saw on the side of the road that night. About a dozen of 'em, they'd pulled down a deer into the ditch just off the shoulder and had set to ripping out mouthfuls of its flank. Looked like they'd been at it for several hours already, come time I drove past 'em in my pickup.

I'm no stranger to wolves, but this was the damnedest thing I'd ever seen. Dad used to take me out hunting back when I was a kid, and we'd come across many a picked-over deer carcass deep into the woods. Always in the woods. Always away from the roadside. If a wolf takes down a deer just off the shoulder, he drags it into the underbrush, away from the metal bears that roar across the asphalt river, away from prying eyes so's he and his pack can feast in peace. Wolves in their world, man in his.

The only time a wolf will come near civilization is if they feel cornered or threatened or if their prey dries up.

A wolf who attacks a full-grown man is either provoked or desperate.

A wolf who attacks a child . . . Well, that's something else entirely.

The pack leader, a large silver wolf with a muzzle slathered in blood, was easy to pick out. Could've been my imagination, or it could've been 'cause I had my high beams on, but I'd swear on my grandfather's grave I saw a glint in one of them wolf's eyes, glowing green a cat's. Odd thing was, only one eye glowed. The other must've been blinded in some scuffle with a rival. Or a hunter.

Whole thing made me glad my .44 Magnum was within easy reach, just in case.

Being stranded in the middle of nowhere with fearless predators just 'round the bend didn't appeal to me, so I stopped at this rundown gas station along Route 77, not far from the reservation border.

Just as I topped off the tank, I heard crying from beyond the trees. This little girl—couldn'a been more'n three or four—came running out the bushes. Ebony braids and torn strips of her dress trailed behind her. Poor thing was bawling her eyes out in the moonlight. Looked like she had some Omaha blood in her. Maybe some Winnebago or Fox.

I didn't notice the blood at first. It covered the front of her dress and trailed down her leg.

She threw herself 'round me and kept sobbing so hard she started hiccupping. "Doggies tried to eat me!" she wailed. "I . . . ran . . . I . . . Please don't let them get me, mister! Please!"

First thing went through my mind was the wolves I'd passed by the side of the road. No telling whether any of 'em were rabid. "Hey, take it easy kid," I said, kneeling. "Everything'll be okay."

In this light, the girl reminded me of my own daughter, back when she was this age.

I picked her up, and she hugged my neck as I wandered inside to pay and ask the attendant if he'd seen anything. The attendant was gone, looked like. Probably out for a smoke.

I carried the girl to the bathroom so's I could try cleaning her up. The wound just above her knee looked no more'n a few minutes old. Teeth marks, damn near right down to the bone. All things considered, she was lucky she could still walk.

"What's your name?" I asked while unrolling some gauze from my truck's first aid kit.

"Emily Howling Coyote," she sniffed, her lip still quivering.

I cleaned the wound with peroxide, but she didn't even flinch. The shock, probably; that'll do that to a kid. "Where are your parents, Emily?" I said.

"Doggies ate 'em," she sobbed. Pointed the direction I had come from.

Great Mystery, had that not been a downed deer?

Picking her up again, I left two twenties on the front counter to pay for my tank of gas and headed back to my truck.

A few steps away from the truck, I caught the green reflection of a single eye hovering just beyond the darkness at the roadside. Similar pairs of wolfish eyes wandered into view, hackles standing on end, black-rimmed teeth bared in open hostility.

Last time I stared down a wolf, I had me a Winchester shotgun. Didn't even have to aim, the choke was so high—and what was left of him limped away to die in the brush somewhere. My father then gave me an eagle feather as proof of my brave warrior spirit, like our ancestors once did.

But that feather was long gone, forgotten somewhere on my road to adulthood. Wore it once at a Sun Dance more'n two decades ago. No idea what happened to it—but I'da given anything to've had it back right then. Mighta made my knees a mite steadier.

I set the girl down behind me so's I could hold my .44 with both hands. "Stay close to me," I said.

More wolves emerged into the light. Six. Eight. Twelve.

I swallowed. My clip only carried eight rounds, and there was no way in hell I could reach my Winchester in the truck without getting mauled first.

Grass rustled behind me. I whirled to find even more eyes, more muzzles, more softly padding paws. We were surrounded.

The first wolf bounded at a low run then darted at full speed, growling and panting the whole way. I took careful aim, held my breath, and filled the night with thunder and gun smoke. The wolf fell into the gravel and slid to a stop right at my feet. The girl yelped and hid behind my leg.

Light left the wolf's eyes. Its ears flagged. Whether or not the beast had been rabid, it upset me just the same. And just as I had done for the other wolf I'd killed when I was a boy, I spoke a silent prayer for the creature.

I am sorry, Grandfather Wolf.

Gravel rattled behind me. I turned and shot down another wolf a few paces away from me. One came at me from the left, another from the right. First shot kicked up a spray of dust. Second shot caught the wolf square in the chest. The other wolf lunged at my leg. The girl shrieked. Teeth buried into my thigh—right where the kid's head shoulda been. The wolf tossed its head from side to side. With both hands I forced the gun barrel against its skull and put a bullet through its brain.

I am sorry, Grandfather Wolf. Forgive me.

Eight wolves left and only three bullets. Great Mystery help us.

One more came at me. The shot missed. Instead of snapping at me, the wolf twisted 'round my injured leg to reach for the girl. This gave me enough time to fire right through its ribcage.

I looked back at her. All this time the wolves kept going after *her*, not me. But why?

Coulda been my imagination, but in the dim light of the filling station sign, I coulda swore I saw a glint in her eye, just like the one I saw in the pack leader's. And I coulda swore I saw her smirking at the wolves I'd killed.

Who *was* this girl?

The other wolves backed off from the circle of light. The silver-tipped pack leader sporting the reddened muzzle of a fresh kill wandered into the clearing. It didn't bare its fangs, and it didn't pounce at me like the others; it just approached with an air of nobility, as though we were chiefs of rival tribes.

This close, I saw it still had both its eyes, but only one of them glowed green.

I lifted the pistol and aimed down the sight. One bullet left. If I could kill the pack leader, the others would surely bolt.

Those eyes—one of polished gold, one of ghostly green fire—stared back at me. *Spoke* to me, not so much with words but with feelings. *You still follow the Old Ways,* they said. *This little one has stolen something from me. Will you help me get it back?*

"Help you? How?"

Step aside, said the wolf.

The most important lesson my late grandmother taught me was this: when the Great Mystery speaks, you damn well better be listening. I looked down at this girl who reminded me of my daughter and realized I had no idea who she really was, what had happened to her parents, or what she coulda stolen from a wolf that could speak right into my thoughts. Powerful forces were at work, forces I might never understand even if I locked myself in a sweat lodge for a month. The Great Mystery had spoken. I had no other choice.

That was when I saw the glee in the girl's snickering face, the unmistakable glow in her eye.

The moment I left the girl's side, the pack leader pounced on her. Nearly three times her size, he bowled her over and bit into her face. Her scream was so loud it echoed across the night sky. The wolf tossed its head from side to side, spraying blood all over the ground, and the screaming silenced. The watery snap made me cringe as the wolf snatched up the little girl's glowing eye into its mouth. It threw its head back and swallowed, licking its chops.

The beast's head turned to regard me once more, this time with a perfect pair of glowing, reflective eyes. *My gratitude, Two-Leg,* the pack leader said. *Coyote the trickster always thinks it funny to steal one of my eyes when I am not looking, but where I am going I will need both. Thank you.*

The girl was gone. Where she had once been, I found nothing more'n a few patches of reddish brown fur—coyote fur, from the look of it. The wolf and his pack were also gone. Only the blood spattered on my clothes spoke to the killing that had just taken place.

After spending the rest of the evening getting my leg stitched up, I awoke the next morning to a rattling outside my trailer. Through the screen door I caught sight of a gray blur darting away into the safety of the trees. As I stepped out in the morning chill to investigate, something tickled my ankle. I looked down. Lying neatly on the welcome mat was a large, black-tipped eagle feather.

SNATCHED AWAY

Sometimes, the right look is all a mark needs to give in. A smoldering glance. Maybe the subtle lifting of one shoulder, curving it towards them at just the right angle. Others, the more difficult marks, require something more tactile. Perhaps the gentle touch of a hand or an accidental graze of a breast against his arm while I'm walking past.

It can be difficult to judge personality at first glance. Some excel at it. Others simply use more tried and true methods without feeling the need to size up their quarry. They take no revelry in their craft, no joy in discovering what makes a man—or sometimes another woman—quiver in their embrace. It comes as no surprise that they are rarely chosen for such sensitive tasks. Someone who bludgeons a mouse to death lacks the finesse of a coiled spring obscured by a nibble of cheese or peanut butter. Foregoing subtlety has its uses, but something about knowing what makes people tick always seems to satisfy.

Those enticed by the eyes see the female form as something to be desired and dominated.

Those lured by touch imagine themselves with the object of their lust and dream of how each sensation in their fantasy will play out.

Those immune to both methods usually require something less tangible.

This method of soul measuring, we call it animometry.

The marks who give in immediately, those who only need the bat of an eyelash or a skintight blouse to betray them, they do not value their virtue. They fill their hollowness with ecstasy only for that insatiable void to return the next morning.

When a target takes longer to respond, it usually means he is waiting for something. Love. Commitment. He likely believes in his so-called virtue and follows some higher road—or leads a different path altogether. Even these are breakable. All it takes is the right trigger.

Put on a few extra pounds. Dye your hair red. Stride around in the right pair of strappy, rhinestone sandals. Bend over in the right pair of denims, with an exposed G-string riding in those magic spots on the hips. Buy him a bottle of his favorite beer.

If none of these work, he is probably into men. And someone else handles that department.

These marks, they never give last names. One-night stands are always on first name basis.

Hey gorgeous, I'm Randy.

Name's Tom. Can I buy you a drink?

The moment a last name comes into the picture, the relationship has entered a new phase. You can look them up in the phonebook. You can call them. And odds are they'll want a two- or three-night stand before their wife catches on.

In my line of work, things never progress past the first night. They can't. The game doesn't work that way.

I've heard every pick-up line ever invented. Those marks who come after me without prompting, before they even say a word, I already know which line they will use.

Hey, I'm parched. Thank God you're a tall drink of water!

Coffee drinker, huh? You want something hot and black inside you?

How about you sit on my lap and we talk about the first thing that pops up?

A response to their vulgarity lets them assume their machismo has worked its spell, that they have the upper hand. Little do they know their delivery of the line means two very important things.

One: My efforts have successfully attracted his attention.

Two: Sex is on the table.

This day and age, there are two radical extremes regarding sex. Many believe copulation is dirty and sinful, an act only suitable for married, heterosexual couples trying to reproduce. Others view sex as a necessary pleasure—the highest attainable bliss—and some spend every waking thought in pursuit of carnal knowledge. The rest fall somewhere in between, balancing across the sword's edge of prudence and pleasure. What neither side realizes is that the sex act creates a metaphysical gateway, a bridge only accessible through one other means.

Death.

The powers that be use this knowledge when assigning me marks.

One such mark, Rick—no last name—was in town for his best friend's wedding and staying at a nearby hotel. His wide shoulders hunkered over a gin and tonic at the hotel bar. The subtle outline of a wedding ring in the pocket of his slacks told me all I needed to know: he fell out of love with his wife long ago and used every out-of-town trip to hunt for whatever sexual escapades he could find. Thankfully, his attempts to seduce any of the bridesmaids to his hotel room had failed miserably at the reception, which made him that much easier to entice.

Simply crossing my legs the right way convinced him to wander my direction.

Within no time, we stumbled into his hotel room. Clothes, abandoned and forgotten on the floor. Hands, groping for sensitive flesh. Genitals, matched and pulsating to the rhythm of ecstasy. Subconsciously, he was using me to punish his wife for tricking him into marrying her. The angry grimace on his face at every rough thrust told me he used sex like violence; the harder he fucked me, the more he would hurt his wife. But it didn't matter.

Rick's entire body writhed just before the end. These cheaters, thieves, child molesters—no matter their crime, their end is always the same. Sweat beading on his red forehead, he wriggled, thrashed, and grunted with one last, hard thrust. His eyes opened wide with surprise. His mouth strained into in a silent scream. And then, just like that, Rick No-last-name collapsed backwards onto the bed, motionless and staring at the ceiling. He would never punish his wife again.

The county coroner would assume Rick had suffered a fatal aneurysm while furiously masturbating. This wouldn't be far from the truth.

When a man ejaculates, his mind empties. For a period of several seconds, he experiences a pleasure so intense that it erases all thoughts. The Japanese call this the Moment of Clouds and Rain, when for a single instant, man touches a higher plane of existence. We call this the rapture point. Only at the moment of the height of ecstasy, a man's soul temporarily leaves his body.

And only then can it be snatched away.

None of us know what the Overseer does with these souls. We merely collect them at the rapture point and return them to the Well. Stories spanning several centuries and from all different cultures say we eat these souls. Some say we come to men in dreams and steal the life from them while they sleep. Others stories tell how we seep into their mind and take over their consciousness, something akin to a demon. In Arabia, the tradition is that we lie in wait in caves so we can destroy men who are unfaithful to their wives by killing them at the first moment of their infidelity.

My favorite story is the one claiming we have teeth in our vaginas.

It doesn't matter how faithful a mark is, how much money he has in the bank, what kind of father he is, whether he's a churchgoer, or when he last donated to charity. We get an assignment. Carry out the assignment. Take our precious cargo back to the Overseer. Some report back immediately; others, like myself, tend to take the scenic route while cradling our hard-fought reward.

Imagine the sound of a thousand, beautiful voices, all singing in perfect harmony and unison. Imagine them singing for you alone, in unending physical delight. This is what cradling a soul feels like.

It is better than euphoric narcotics. Better than sex.

And then we return home to drop the shining ball of pleasure into the bottomless Well and leave in search of our next mark—if only to enjoy that pleasure just one more time.

Delilah, one of the best hunters I've ever had the privilege of working with, is convinced the feeling is manufactured simply so we will continue on the hunt, much like how nature designed procreation to be pleasurable. Without ecstasy and instinct, would humanity ever produce children, even by accident? Doubtful. Delilah always felt the need to associate delight with guilt. Nothing that feels good could ever be natural, she says. But she tags the biggest bounties. A little hypocritical, maybe? Perhaps, but at least she gets the job done. Case in point: her three highest-profile marks were hunters just like myself. No one else could manage to bring down, but she did somehow.

If anyone comes after me, it will probably be her.

My last mark I met several years ago in—of all places—a laundromat.

Just as a few of the right questions can lead to the Achilles heel, the same can be said about the venue in which the quarry is found. The man who watches women gyrate at strip clubs is sexually frustrated. The guy at the local watering hole can probably be plied with alcohol. Even in such a mundane place as a bar, *where* he is sitting tells me more about him than he might ever guess. If he's on a barstool, he's probably seeking a sympathetic ear. If he's sitting alone in a smoky corner, he probably thinks none of the women there will pay attention to him, but he hopes in silence. If he's dancing like a fool after just a few drinks, he doesn't care what other people think about him.

So what does a laundromat say about someone other than implicating a standard human need for clean clothes and the lack of a functioning washer and dryer at home? It could imply that he was a person of meager means, that the quarters he fed into each machine were difficult to part with.

Souls down on their luck present no challenge. This type usually responds to the sugar mommy complex. Pretend to be a long-lost friend who has just inherited a fortune. Or act like some rich fuck who has grown a guilty conscience due to a religious experience and feels obligated to philanthropize one destitute person after another. Someone who's worn the same pair of shoes for three or four years or who has half a dozen starving kids at home will take anything from a stranger. Food, clothing, money. Especially money. They'll believe any lie we throw at them so long as they get something in return. So I'll tell them I'm Bonnie from university or that I'm a religious nutjob with five million just burning a hole in my Swiss bank account. Those kind of people eat that shit up.

But this mark . . . something was different about him. Maybe it was a certain glint in his eyes that hinted at a kind of hope the downtrodden rarely have. Maybe it was the way he carried himself, not with confidence per se but a kind of humble surety. Most impoverished people lack that kind of posture: their spines tend to possess a slight curvature at the neck since they have long ago stopped looking to the skies. This mark, though, he stood with a more regal bearing. A prince in pauper's clothes.

Whatever it was, an invisible thread stronger than my orders or my desire to hold another soul tugged me in his direction.

Most of my marks tend to fall into two categories. Arrogant men tend to hate women, cheat on their wives, and think they are entitled to everything they see. Downcast men tend to hate themselves, are single, and will latch onto any kind of feminine attention they're given.

This man fell into neither camp.

He casually smiled at me when I passed him to use the change machine, which indicated he wasn't a misogynist. There was no ring on his finger, which implied he wasn't married. He was, however, alone.

The easiest marks are always alone.

After shoving his clothes in the nearest empty dryer, he picked up a little black notebook and started writing in it while he waited. From peering over his shoulder, I could make out what looked like notes for some kind of story.

The usual venues provide an easy opening. In a strip club, the men come to me; no need to do anything other than wear the right outfit (or lack thereof). At a bar, it's not out of the ordinary these days for a woman to buy a guy a drink. How, then, does one pick up a date at a laundromat?

Pretending the spinning dryer next to his was mine, I sidled up next to him and struck up a friendly conversation. His name was Peter, I soon found out. He never told me his last name, but the way he looked me in the eyes said he desperately wanted to.

We stood and shot the shit for a while—nothing titillating or overtly suggestive, just casual banter. And all the while, his eyes kept flitting back to the closed notebook harbored in his hands, as though all this talk was keeping him from something important. The whole time, I dropped subtle hints into the conversation—ex-boyfriend, having nothing to do on a Friday night, being new to the area, and so on.

No matter what I did, he still wouldn't bite.

These types of marks were always the toughest kind to crack. These kind need rapport before you can get them in the sack.

For several months, our laundry schedules just happened to coincide. Each day, the mark would greet me with a bigger smile. Each week, he seemed more genuinely happy to see me. His little black notebook evolved into a large, spiral-bound journal, then a folder of loose leaves stained with red corrections.

Over time, I started thinking of him more as "Peter" than "the mark." I would follow him to his one-bedroom apartment unseen and watch him live alone in a rather solitary existence—never going to parties, rarely inviting friends over. But that is not to say he had nothing to show for it.

Peter wasn't just down on his luck. He was poor by choice.

Everything about his whole life was beautiful. From the stories he wrote to the music he played on his piano to the paintings he hung on his walls, it all set me to wondering.

What had Peter done to deserve his soul being snatched away before his time? Nothing. He hadn't cheated on a wife or stolen from an employer or molested children or any number of despicable crimes which warranted such a sentence. As far as I could tell, Peter exemplified the perfect human being.

Order were orders, however. Knowing Peter would take a while to crack still meant he needed to crack eventually, as Delilah so often liked to remind me.

She stopped to check in with me every once in a while. She would tell me about all of her current exploits—the sudden heart attack of a corrupt CEO and the death of an affluent widower caught philandering with a prostitute, the most recent rogue sister she'd hunted down—and she would describe which of her latest marks had provided her the best sex in recent memory. Normal girl talk.

Before flying off to her next conquest, she would waggle a finger in my face and admonish me about slacking off.

"I know what you're doing, Sis," she would say, tossing her black hair, flashing me those same seductive green eyes she used to turn men's self-control into jelly. "If you're not careful, this case just might be taken away from you. Other sisters might be more . . . persuasive. And you don't want to end up like poor Rebecca, now, do you?"

Delilah was right, as always. For whatever reason, Peter's soul required collecting. Some nights, I would follow him home, trying to figure out what chink in his armor I hadn't yet exploited. I would fantasize about the sex we would have and dream about what holding his snatched soul would feel like. How would it vibrate differently from the others? At what pitch would that choir of thousands sing for eternity in my ears?

The chink was so easy to see once I thought outside the picture frame. And outside that frame, I discovered a way to eliminate two problems at once.

Delilah's latest mark was also giving her some trouble. A fifty-something book editor at a large publishing house—who happened to control an extensive underground pornography operation—would not respond to anything she threw at her. She could prop herself up on top of his desk with her panties dangling from one foot, and he wouldn't even pop an erection. It wasn't until I read one of Peter's novel manuscripts that an idea struck me.

Peter loved writing about women. He always employed strong female protagonists, often dealt with common women's issues, and frequently included prominent lesbian characters that were unashamed of their sexuality. His latest book included some tasteful scenes where two women engaged in threesomes with a town councilman in order to trick him into voting down a council measure.

I convinced Peter to submit the novel and told him I had the perfect publisher in mind. Peter submitted the manuscript to Delilah's mark, and within a few days she discovered the editor loved the piece—mostly due to the more provocative scenes, I assumed—and had already sent Peter a message offering a three-book deal.

It had been a long time since I'd dealt with a man who couldn't get it up unless he had *two* women in front of him. Before the editor could draft a formal publishing contract, Delilah and I met with him and presented a counteroffer he couldn't resist.

If he refused to buy Peter's manuscript, Delilah and I would live in his bed for a month.

Naturally, I was wearing the kind of black leather stilettos that drove him wild when I presented the idea.

Naturally, the "month" ended after his first orgasm. Delilah collected his soul and flew off to deposit it in the Well with all the other choirs.

The next time I saw Peter, it was raining outside. Notebooks or manuscript pages were nowhere to be found.

"I'd have been better off saving my quarters and letting my laundry sit outside," he said.

Peter wasn't worried about the money. He believed one day humanity would look through the eyes of his characters and see the same world he did. That an esteemed editor went from passionate to disinterested in a matter of days hit Peter harder than a swift kick to the testicles.

Or at least that's what my animometry told me; he never said much about it.

All he said while watching the rain was, "You wanna get a cup of coffee or something?"

When a man invites you to get a cup of coffee, you know it will eventually end up in sex a few dates down the road.

First, coffee. Then lunch. Dinner. Nightcaps, if he's not a teetotaler.

Everyone, deep down, desires some kind of sexual fulfillment whether they acknowledge it or not. Even people who actively deny their libido—priests, nuns, those who have taken a vow of celibacy for personal reasons, or those who believe sex is a tool of Satan or whatever religious antagonist they believe in—even they cannot destroy humanity's most powerful impulse forever. Sex means so many different things to different people, but even for those that deny it for whatever reason, once the boulder starts rolling down the mountainside, only someone with titanium willpower can stand in its way and survive being flattened.

Killing Peter's willpower had certainly done the trick. Instead of sharing his ideas, he closed in on himself. The light in his eyes faded. His smile darkened. Some people cope with loss or bad turns of events in completely different ways. Some drink themselves silly. Some kill themselves. Overeat. Spend too much money. Withdraw from society. Fuck anything that moves. They will do anything to force themselves not to think about what they had lost.

Peter, he grabbed the object of his worship and refused to let go. At last, the time was right.

But the night we ended up in each other's arms, his eyes spoke a language I had never heard. Without saying a word, he became a deer that voluntarily stepped out into oncoming headlights. I saw in his eyes the unmistakable look of someone committing suicide. Sad. Determined. Scared shitless. And still he went through with it.

Being on top is the best position. Not only can a woman control the rhythm and depth, if a mark somehow intuits what is happening, there is no way he can pull out and escape his fate. He cannot wriggle free, and I can ride him hard enough to guarantee a rapture point extraction before he can fight me off.

Sometimes when I am on top, my body relaxes. My wings unfurl from their tight folds below my shoulder blades and spread out to catch an imaginary gust of wind. My tail uncoils to tickle his scrotum. Granted, these are aspects normal eyes cannot see. In all of my days, only one man saw my true form: a widowed Methodist pastor starved for sex.

With me on top, Peter gazed past my breasts, past my hair, as though he could see my featherless wings hovering above us. His motion stopped. He sank back into the sheets and stared overhead, then back at my face.

"I knew it," he whispered between ragged breaths. "I knew you were here for me."

My whole body shivered. How could he have known? Had someone warned him? Did he have eyes like that pastor's, from so long ago?

"And yet you gave in anyway," I said, more of a statement than a question. The excitement flared up inside me remained constant. Even more than I wanted to carry away his soul, I needed to continue. I needed to finish.

I needed *him*.

"Is that so hard to believe?" His eyes welled up with tears. "How can a man escape his own destiny when an angel comes to take him away?"

Angel? I shuddered and pulled away from him. Off him. "No," I said. "You have this all wrong. I'm not—"

He pressed a finger over my lips and pulled me closer to him. "Angel, demon, temptress—It doesn't matter what you are. Take me with you."

My mind spun. A hardened criminal never turns himself in to the police.

I was an executioner, yet Peter had committed no crime. There were no spurned ex-lovers waiting in the wings to cast the first stone, no broken hearts that retribution would mend.

Somehow, my animometrics had been wrong. No, my *assignment* was wrong. Though fairy tales paint us as sex-starved creatures that kill for unholy pleasure, in all of my long memory, I have never taken a soul at whim. I was not about to extract a soul I was unsure of. Extraction is permanent. Once a soul is severed, that gossamer thread tying it to the body cannot be reconnected.

And there was something else, something about the way he searched my face, how he gazed upon my wings with wonder and longing. For the first time since first meeting him, I pictured how the world would change if his dream succeeded. How *he* would change. How *I* would change.

The world would be a much darker place without him in it.

With both hands, I pushed myself from him and fought to regain my breath.

Peter's dazed eyes met my own with sadness. "What is wrong?"

"I can't," I told him. "If you finish inside me, you will die."

"Then let me. I don't belong here."

"Don't you?" My wings folded beneath my shoulder blades as I sat back against the headboard and covered myself with the sheets. "Let me tell you a story."

Humans do not remember their first few years of life. I, however, remember everything since my moment of conception. My first memory consists of swimming in a black pool and feeling a tug from somewhere outside myself. I had no name, and yet I stepped into existence knowing everything I would ever need to learn.

My first assignment targeted a traitorous architect in the court of Egyptian pharaoh Thutmose III. Since then, I have lost count of how many souls I've escorted to the Well. And yet, with all of my past experience, with all of the tricky men I had seduced to my bed throughout the ages, I could not bring myself to collect such a simple and easy mark as Peter.

Once Peter understood my story, I unfurled my wings and flew across the black sky, beyond the clouds, the moon, the stars. My mind could not rest, not until I knew the right choice to make.

The Well sits at the base of an endless staircase of starlight. By human reckoning, it stretches a mile across, encircled by a rim of wavering moonlight. So many times I have stood at its edge and gazed down—not into water but an endless abyss of nothingness. So many times I have wondered what lies at the bottom. Did it lead to a different world, where the punished souls received their just rewards? Would some cataclysmic event happen once the brim overflowed with shining grains of sand? Sometimes I imagined a giant machine with a huge wheel, whereupon every harvested soul slogged in chains to make the wheel turn. This wheel, this machine made the whole universe work.

I stood at the foot of the starlit steps, just barely able to make out the shrouded shape at the distant top of the staircase. While I awaited acknowledgement, dozens of other colleagues glided overhead to drop a brightly glowing soul into the Well.

"You have made good progress," the Overseer's voice drifted down from the above. "I knew he would be exceptionally difficult, but you have assured me my faith in your skills was not misplaced. He will break soon."

"Thank you, Master," I said, dropping to one knee. "But is his extraction entirely necessary?"

The shape rose abruptly. Even as distant as he was, the Overseer grew three times in size. "How dare you! I did not call you from the black to disobey!"

I shrank from his furor. "But he has committed no crime! How is his death punishment?"

"Child," the Overseer said, his voice softening as he rested back into his throne, "what if I told you that allowing him to live would lead an entire nation to ruin? His words are charismatic. The first person to espouse his beliefs will speak to others. The one becomes two; the two, four; the four, eight. This will incite war which will rage for decades. What good is one man's soul if it saves billions more from damnation?"

Tears melted my face. The logic was irrefutable. "But—I love him!" I blurted without thinking. As soon as the words left my lips, they became true. All these centuries I'd heard the word "love," yet not until I pictured a world without Peter in it did the meaning behind that unshakable fear make sense to me.

I *loved* him.

I expected the Overseer to scold me for this outburst, maybe to sentence me to my imagined wheel for a few centuries. Instead, he sank back, quiet and contemplative. "We have all sacrificed love for greater things, my child," he said, a mere whisper of regret. "Do this one thing, and I will ensure you want for nothing."

Hesitation set in. How could I want for nothing if the only thing I desired was thrown out of reach forever?

"Will you complete your assignment?" he asked again.

Swallowing the anxious lump in my throat, I gazed up into the starry eyes of the one who had called me forth from darkness. "Yes, Master," I said and took flight.

Peter was dozing beneath tossed sheets when I arrived. He seemed just as peaceful in repose as he did when awake. How could a gentle soul such as he possibly provoke war? He wrote stories about love and beauty, and for this he would destroy whole nations?

Surely not.

As he slept, I read his soul again, just to be sure. Colors—such vibrant colors!—radiated from within, swirling in a effervescent wash of light. Streaks of brown, gray, or black usually mar the average mark's essence, but Peter's animistic kaleidoscope shone as brightly as sunlight reflected through a morning dewdrop.

There was only one thing to do.

When a man is told his life is in danger, he will act quickly no matter what state of sleep—or lack thereof—he is in. If he believes someone is actively trying to kill him, he will gather up his wallet and keys, put on some shoes, and drive off into the dawn before you can say rapture point. He will move two states over, reconnect with an estranged aunt, and check into a nearby hotel.

A few marks try to run from their pursuers. Some get it into their minds that we have nefarious plans for them, and they take off in the night before our charms can snake them out of their pants. In some cases, we track them down and apply good old fashioned coercion. In more sensitive situations, the primary hunter tracks the mark down, and a more sympathetic hunter moves in to finish the job. Regardless of who performs the extraction, whoever makes first contact with the subject could follow him to the furthest reaches of the universe if necessary.

No matter where Peter went, I could find him.

That night, in a different bed, in a different city, we made love again. And the next night. And the night after. I couldn't ever let him finish. No matter how much I desired him, I could make no guarantee that instinct wouldn't force me to snatch up his soul out of habit.

We went on like this for days. Weeks. Maybe even years—it was hard to tell. He spent his days writing freelance articles for local newspapers, scratching up enough cash to live out of cheap motels, and at night he tried his best to understand me in every way he could.

I told myself I wasn't disobeying orders. I would collect Peter's soul *eventually*, just on a timetable of my choosing. The longer, the better.

Why is it that people only rationalize their questionable choices to themselves and to others when they already believe what they are doing is wrong to begin with?

One blustery autumn evening, Peter came home with a photograph. "I met someone today who says she knows you," he said and handed me the picture.

A beautiful face with haunting green eyes and teased black hair stared back at me.

My face went white.

"Said her name was Delilah," he said. "You know her?"

The photograph dropped from my hand.

"Don't worry," he said, picking up the picture from the floor. "I didn't tell her where you were. Something seemed funny about her."

In the millennia since my summoning, several hunters out of countless multitudes have willfully abandoned their assignments, but each new hunter learns about three cases in particular, three ways in which a hunter could fall off of her bike. A veteran named Tamar was already considered ancient by our standards when I came forth from the black. She ranked among the best of us, yet one day she disappeared with her latest prey instead of claiming his soul. The second, a young hunter called Rebecca, would spend weeks lazing about, doing nothing, but before her self-imposed vacation, she was perhaps the best hunter of us all. The third, Selene, had extracted a soul but refused to bring it to the Well. She sheltered the soul in her hands for the better part of a decade, drifting from location to location like a junkie on a constant high while holding onto a never-ending orgasm.

Everyone agreed Tamar was simply too old and should have faded into the ether long ago; Rebecca, on the other hand, probably hadn't been put together right from the beginning. Selene had extracted so many souls in so short a time that she became addicted to holding souls, and each new hunt no longer satisfied her.

Although hunters rebelled and were stopped on an occasional basis, Tamar, Rebecca, and Selene were special cases because the Overseer sent hunter after hunter to bring his wayward children to heel, and none had returned.

None but Delilah, that is.

In all of these worst-case scenarios, she had dragged the deserters kicking and screaming to the Overseer's throne. Normal rogue hunters who were hunted down simply earned the immediate disruption of their physical and spiritual form, but for costing the Overseer so much time and trouble, he ordered all three offenders to be cast into the Well without question.

Our master gifted my brothers and sisters with thought, reason, and emotion, but he did not give us souls like the humans have. Without knowing the Well's purpose, I could only guess what fate befell Tamar, Rebecca, and Selene, as three soulless beings thrown into a machine intended for souls. Back then, I liked to think they were stuck in a limbo where they could watch all of the precious souls around them but would never again be able to hold one. Knowing Delilah was on my trail, I wanted to believe Tamar, Rebecca, and Selene faded from existence the moment they disappeared past the Well's alabaster rim. Delilah was the best of us. She could seduce a man or woman with the simplest of things. Her extraction count ranked higher than anyone. If the three worst-case rogues had failed to elude her, what chance did I have?

Peter gathered me into his arms. That slaughterhouse lamb look returned to his eyes. Did he somehow know this might be our last chance?

To that end, I abandoned my usual caution. This time I made love to him to *save* his life, not to take it. We clasped hands. My wings folded around him like a second set of arms. My tail coiled around his leg, never to let go, as I lost myself to the kind of abandon I could only find in his arms. Our love blazed fast and urgent atop the sheets.

In the midst of heady bliss, Peter's body shuddered beneath me in the throes of delight. He was close; I could feel it. But as I tried to pull myself away from him, his arms would not let me go. He thrust and shivered one last time before laying back, limp.

I opened my eyes to find Delilah hovering before us, her eyes twisted in ecstasy. Between her fingers, a tiny grain of sand glistened brighter than a full moon seen through winter crystal. That tiny filament of silver connected to the center of Peter's chest.

"Stupid girl," she said. "I knew you'd never finish this one."

I reached out to snatch the soul from her. She yanked it from my reach, and the cord snapped.

Peter's body lay silent, forever. Not "the mark." Not "the prey."

Peter.

Hot tears trickled down my cheeks. My wings cradled him.

"Are you going to turn me in?" I asked. "Or have our years

working together counted for nothing?"

"There's no need," she smirked, eyeing the soul in her palm while shivering with visible ecstasy. "I have a feeling you'll do exactly what you must."

Delilah blew me a kiss, and just like that, the darkness whisked her away.

Even though Peter's soul had departed his body, a tingle in the back of my mind pointed the way. There was still time. I let go of Peter's cold body—it was, after all, just a shell—and leaped into the heavens high enough for my wings to catch air. Peter's face burned into my memory, spurring my flight faster and faster.

I was waltzing right into a trap, but that no longer mattered. I feared more for what would happen to him than for my own fate.

The earthly veil parted into a world of stars, and the Well's vast rim spread out before me. Above, dozens of my peers flanked the Overseer. Surrounded me.

Sister Sapphira. Sister Jezebel. Vashti. Magdalene. Brothers Adonis and Abbadon.

Delilah hovered at the front of them, just above the Well. Peter's soul shimmered and gleamed in her palm as though light was its only language. She passed the trophy around from one sister to another. Each one touched him, tongues lolling about in pleasure, eyes rolling back into their heads. Forced to stand and watch, I understood the mind of a jealous lover.

Our master's tone surprised me with its softness. "Thank you for allowing Delilah to finish her mission," he said. "You were the only one of my children who could get close enough to complete this task, but I knew before I even sent you that you were not strong enough to do it alone."

My throat constricted in the face of intense scrutiny. I had defied my orders only to endure my sisters' reproving stare and watch them fondle the object of my affection.

"Your efforts are not without merit," he continued. "Because of your cooperation with Delilah, this man will no longer threaten reality as we know it."

Delilah once told me there comes a single moment in every hunter's existence where she wonders about the nature of her purpose. Most are able to provide themselves an answer in short order. Others, like Tamar and Rebecca, dwell on the question until it burrows into their essence and destroys whatever spark of motivation they once possessed. This moment, Delilah said, is designed to come only once. Sometimes it arrives early, when we are so fresh from the black that the whole world seems a jumble. Other times it rears its head late in the game, when we are so entrenched in our ways that contemplating the meaning of life can send us over the edge.

This was my time. Peter had planted the seed, but it had not flowered until I witnessed his soul being passed amongst my brothers and sisters for their own personal enjoyment.

Standing there before my master and my siblings, the logic crystallized. Either all harvested souls had committed some grave sin, or the Overseer had been deceiving me all of these past millennia.

Peter was blameless.

My master had misled me for the last time.

The shining soul passed back around to Delilah, who stroked her cheek against the shining light.

Delilah, back when I'd asked, told me her conflict of purpose had lasted no more than a flash of lightning across a thundercloud, long before I was ever called forth. Watching her then—eyes rolled back into her head, the tip of her tongue hanging from the corner of her mouth—it became clear to me that her purpose did not concern itself with ethics so long as she could experience pleasure.

I took to the air, hovering above the Well, and confronted the hunter I often thought of as the closest thing my kind could call a friend. My teeth ground in my jaw.

"Give—him—back."

Her derisive cackle startled me. "And why should I do such a thing?"

"He's *mine*."

"Is he now?" she smirked. "You're mistaken. All souls belong to the Well. Humans only borrow them for a time, and we are responsible for extracting and bringing them back."

"Is that the lie you've been telling yourself since you had your conflict of purpose, to keep from addling like Tamar or Selene?" I frowned. "If you hadn't been so afraid of what you carried all these years, perhaps you would have taken the time to realize there is more to our purpose than chasing after the next mark."

Delilah bared her teeth. "I am done with you. *All* of us are done with you." She held out her glowing hand. "If this really is yours—if you really want it—then you'll have to go after it."

And just like that, she overturned her palm.

The grain of sand sparkled as it tumbled out of her grasp. Down. Down towards the Well.

My mind was already made up.

Better a slave with love than free with nothing.

So I dove after him. I dove right down into the Well, faster than I had ever dived before, without considering the consequences, pushing Tamar, Rebecca, and Selene's fates from my mind. I had eyes only for the tiny falling star just out of reach.

Within the blackness, he was the only thing I could see. He was my Polaris, my North. Alone at the gates of oblivion, together. Was there a better end?

My last ounce of strength reached out for him further than I'd ever thought possible. As my hand closed around him, the choirs filled my head. The sensation came to me as if angels sang from several realities away, but it no longer mattered as I clutched him to my chest, unable to let go.

Reaching out to grab him had robbed my wings of air, and no matter how hard I tried, they failed to gain enough lift to pull out of my dive. Even before diving, I knew this had been a one-way trip. Instead of focusing on the all-consuming blackness below, I studied Peter's essence.

If a soul pulsates strongly, it is usually livid and angry at being removed from its host. If it shines weakly, it has given up and resigned itself to its fate. If it waxes and wanes, it is confused and disoriented. Peter's light, however, remained solid, his vibration and pitch unwavering, as though he knew I was the one sheltering him from the ravages of my sisters, from the chains awaiting us at the wheel driving the Well.

In our last moments, he seemed content, and a smile worked its way across my face. Surely there was no better way to meet the end.

But that end never came.

I found myself naked in an alley. Peter's soul was nowhere nearby, but something felt different. I could sense him somehow but could neither see nor touch him. Suddenly a sobering, cold ocean swelled up inside me. I felt . . . full. Whole, like an endless world of possibilities had been opened up to me. And then I understood.

The Well of souls was indeed a wheel—just not the kind I had always imagined. Like a spinning wheel turns cotton, flax, or wool into thread, so the Well took the castoffs of humanity and turned them into something more, something usable. Me, a being called forth without a soul, had melded with one. Falling through the Well had fused Peter into an inseparable part of me.

This meant Tamar and Rebecca and Selene were all out there somewhere, struggling to fit in with the very society they once preyed upon. I had lived in this world for so long and yet never had anyone besides Peter whom I could call a friend. All I could think about was finding my sisters who had been banished to this mortal realm.

A local shelter provided me with clothes and a place to stay. A careful campaign waged in local bars provided more than enough sugar-daddy fees from short flings to get myself back on my feet. It felt strange at first, copulating without stealing a shining grain of sand at the climax of passion. Sleeping with the same person more than once took even further getting used to.

Within a week, I found myself back at Peter's apartment, alone. The place lay just as we had left it, in a state of hurried disarray. Even as torn up as it was, the tiny abode came as close to feeling like a home to me as possible. In a corner of discarded books and clothes, I discovered several of Peter's old notebooks and folders. Before long, I found myself writing in them whenever the task of searching for my sisters did not distract me. After a time, I began writing drafts from Peter's notes.

For good or for ill, whatever aspect of Peter's soul the Overseer had sought to erase by dropping him in the Well had survived intact by my shielding presence.

One night, I returned from a meeting with an editor and found a note on my pillow:

You were right.
—D

Delilah had already experienced her conflict of purpose, and even though she had been lying to herself all these millennia, her nature would never give her another chance to follow in my footsteps. If the Overseer has ordered her to hunt me down for what I had done, she will have no choice but to comply.

Instinct tells me they will leave me be, at least for now. Delilah won't risk exposing herself in all-out war just to get to me. Besides, I know all of her tactics, all of her tricks. No one, not even beauties like Abbadon or Adonis, can hope to bed me and steal the soul I had fought so hard to hold onto.

One word at a time, I complete Peter's masterpieces. Works of beauty, poetry, love. Let these words lead nations to war, I say. Let the hunters come for me; they will not prevail.

After all, the easiest marks are always alone, and I'm not alone anymore.

ACKNOWLEDGEMENTS

It takes a number of people to put a finished book in someone's hands, but it takes far more to forge a writer capable of writing said book. The following are among the many to whom I owe a debt of gratitude:

My late cousin Derek, without whom I probably would never have gone down this road. I still miss you.

My parents, for supporting me every step of the way.

Ron Marz, who gave me my first taste of the dos and don'ts of publishing.

Ed Davis, for showing me the ropes of the publishing industry.

Carrie Landers, for slogging through the early drafts with me and pushing me to keep going.

Jason Schmetzer, for buying my very first story and opening up the doors to a larger world.

Gery Deer and the Western Ohio Writers Association, for providing a wonderful support system for a lonely profession.

Bill Bicknell, for an insightful edit.

Michael Martin and Matt Heerdt, for a fantastic cover.

And lastly, Mr. Wil Wheaton, who was a bright point of light during a particularly dark time. I'm still following your advice.

ABOUT THE AUTHOR

PHILIP A. LEE has written extensively for the gaming industry, including the *BattleTech*, *Cosmic Patrol*, and *Shadowrun* universes. He lives in Dayton, Ohio, with his significant other and their three cats. You can learn more about his work at PHILIPLEEWRITING.COM.